A Bravo Christmas Reunion

CHRISTINE RIMMER

MILLS & BOON®
Pure reading pleasure™

First published in Great Britain 2008
Large Print edition 2008
Harlequin Mills & Boon Limited,
Eton House, 18-24 Paradise Road,
Richmond, Surrey TW9 1SR

ISBN: 978 0 263 20151 2

Set in Times Roman 17¼ on 23¼ pt.
35-1208-49528

Printed and bound in Great Britain
by CPI Antony Rowe, Chippenham, Wiltshire

CHRISTINE RIMMER

came to her profession the long way around. Before settling down to write about the magic of romance, she'd been everything, including an actress, a salesclerk and a waitress. Now Christine is grateful not only for the joy she finds in writing, but for what waits when the day's work is through: a man she loves, who loves her right back and the privilege of watching their children grow and change day to day. She lives with her family in Oklahoma. Visit Christine at her new home on the web at www.christinerimmer.com

For Betty Lowe, lifelong friend and
loyal reader, what endures is the
laughter, the caring, the sharing.
In the end, there is always love.

Chapter One

Marcus Reid knew damn well that he should stay away from Hayley Bravo. Far, far away.

Since she dumped him and left Seattle, he'd worked harder than ever, rising before dawn to push his body to the limit in his personal gym, burning the midnight oil at the office, driving himself to exhaustion every day. Evenings when he didn't have to be at his corporate headquarters, he kept himself good and busy. He dated, making it a point to get out more—with gorgeous, attentive, appreciative women. Women more glamorous than Hayley, women more sophisticated than Hayley. Agreeable women. Women who had sense enough not to ask the impossible of him.

Yeah. It had taken him months to get over Hayley. A lot longer, if you wanted the hard truth, than he'd expected. Getting over Hayley had turned out to be one hell of a job. Almost as hard as dealing with his ex-wife Adriana's final desertion.

But he'd managed it.

Or so he kept telling himself. *He was over Hayley*. Done. Finished.

So why was he standing on the doorstep of her Sacramento apartment on that cold evening in mid-December?

Since Marcus had no intention of answering that particular question, he banished it from his mind with a shake of his head.

The complex she lived in was perfectly ordinary, built around a central courtyard, the boxy units accessed from outside. Low to midrange in price, he would guess. She'd lived a lot better when she worked for him. He'd seen to it. Not only a fat salary, but a big expense account and a luxury car, compliments of his company, Kaffe Central. And then there were the gifts he'd showered on her....

Now she was on her own, she'd be watching her budget. That bothered him, the thought of her pinching pennies to get along. Though their relationship had ended, some part of him still wanted to take care of her.

Light glowed in the window to the left of her door. Through the partly open blinds, he could see she had put up a Christmas tree. And he could hear music, faintly. A Christmas song?

Hayley was into the Christmas crap big-time. Strings of lights twined on the railing of her second floor landing, where she'd made herself a sort of patio with a couple of wicker chairs and a wooden crate for a table. A miniature tree, tiny lights twinkling, topped the crate—and he was stalling, checking out her Christmas decorations instead of getting on with it.

Time to make a move. Ring the bell. Or get the hell out of there.

He sucked in a big breath, lifted his hand and gave her doorbell a punch.

After a few never-ending seconds, the door swung wide. The music from inside swelled louder: "White Christmas."

And there she was, the light from behind her haloing her red hair. Those eyes that managed to be blue and gray and green all at once went wide with surprise. And a bright smile died unborn on that mouth that he'd loved to kiss.

"Marcus!" Her expression was not encouraging. Far from it. She looked…pained. Slightly panicked, even. She brought her hand to her mouth and then lowered it—to her stomach.

He tracked the movement, watched as her palm settled on the round shape of her belly, fingers curving gently. Protectively. He stared at her pale hand and the roundness beneath it, trying to accept what he saw.

It was…enormous, her stomach. It looked as if she had a beach ball tucked in there, beneath the tentlike red sweater she wore.

Too stunned to fake politeness, he shut his gaping mouth—and then opened it again to accuse roughly, "You're pregnant." He lifted his gaze and met her eyes again.

She was frowning, more worried now than panicked. "Marcus. Are you okay? You look—"

"I'm fine." Outright lie. His stomach churned, spurting acid. He needed to hit someone. Preferably whatever bastard had dared to put his hands on her, to do *that* to her.

God. Hayley with some other guy, having that other guy's baby…

It didn't seem possible. He couldn't believe it.

At the same time as he knew this couldn't be happening, some rational part of his mind saw clearly the ridiculousness of his disbelief. Why the hell *wouldn't* she be with some other guy? Some guy who made her happy. Some guy who loved her and cherished her and wanted to make a family with her….

"White Christmas" ended. Bells jingled as "Winter Wonderland" came next.

"Marcus…" She reached out a hesitant hand. "Please come in and—"

He cut her off by moving back just slightly, out of the way of her touch.

"Oh, Marcus…" She looked at him with what might have been pity.

He wanted to shout at her then, tell her loud and clear that she never, ever had to feel sorry for him. But he didn't shout. Far from it. Instead, he said what he'd planned to say. He doled out the stock phrases, just to show her that finding her big as a house with some other guy's kid didn't affect him in the least.

"I'm in town on business. Thought I'd stop by, see how you're doing…."

She wrapped her arms around herself, resting them on that impossible belly, and looked at him steadily. Now those eyes of hers looked sad. "I'm all right."

He parodied a smile. "Great. Did I catch you having dinner?"

She pressed her lips together and shook her head.

He craned to the side, hoping to see beyond her into the apartment. "Your, uh, husband home?"

She took forever to answer. Finally, so gently, she told him, "No, Marcus."

He waited, his gaze on her face, carefully *not* glancing down again at her bulging stomach.

Finally she heaved a big sigh. "Look. Are you coming in or not?"

"Yeah."

She stepped back. He crossed the threshold. She shut the door, closing the two of them in that apartment together.

The place was small. Straight ahead a hallway led into shadow. To the right was a narrow kitchen with a tiny two-seater table. On the left was the living room area. There, the brightly lighted tree already had a pile of festively wrapped presents beneath it. The TV cabinet dripped garland and fake red berries. She even had a Nativity scene on one of the side tables.

Leave it to Hayley to do Christmas full out. Last December, she'd…

But he wasn't going to think about last December. Last December was gone. Over. Done. He was only here to say hi and wish her and her baby—and the guy, too, damn him to hell, whoever he was—a nice life.

"Your coat," she suggested softly, reaching out.

He dodged her touch again. "It's all right. I'll keep it on."

She dropped her outstretched arm. "Okay." It was her turn to fake a smile. "Well. Have a seat." She indicated the blue couch in the living room. Obediently, he marched over there and sat down.

"A drink?" she offered, still hovering there on the square of tile that served as her entrance hall.

He realized a drink sounded pretty damn good. He *needed* a drink at a moment like this. Something to numb his senses, blur his vision. Something to make it so he didn't care that Hayley was having someone else's kid. "Great. Thanks."

"Pepsi?"

"No. A real drink. Anything but whiskey."

She blinked. She knew how he felt about booze, as a rule. "Well, sure. I think I've got some vodka around here. No tonic or anything, though..."

"Vodka. Some ice. Whatever."

She turned toward the kitchen. He watched her in there as she got down a glass. She disappeared for a moment. He heard ice cubes clinking. And then she was back in his line of vision, glass in one hand, a bottle in the other. She poured the clear liquor over the ice, put the lid back on the bottle and came to him, that belly of hers leading the way.

"Thanks," he said, when she handed it over. He knocked it back in one swallow and held out the glass again. "Another."

She opened her beautiful mouth to speak—but he glared at her and she said nothing. Silent but for a sigh, she took the glass and waddled back to the counter, where she poured him a second one. She approached again and held out the glass. He took it. And then he watched with bleak fascination as she moved to a chair across from him and carefully lowered herself into it.

The liquor, thankfully, had no smell. He considered knocking back the second glass. But he had a feeling if he did, it might just come right back up again. So he sipped the disgusting stuff slowly and told himself to be grateful that it had no more taste that it had smell, just a slight unpleasant oiliness on the tongue.

She asked, her chin tipped high, "How did you know where I live?"

"I kept track of you." Did he sound like some stalker? He qualified, "Just your address. Your phone number…" It was nothing obsessive, he'd told himself. But he did feel a certain… responsibility for her. He'd hired someone to get her address and phone number after she left him.

And about that phone number? More than once, when he was pretty sure she wouldn't be home, he'd dialed that number, just to hear her voice on her answering machine and know that if he needed to get in touch with her again, he could.

"I wanted to be sure," he said, "that you were doing okay."

"Well." She lifted both hands, as if to indicate everything around her—the cramped apartment, the blue couch he sat on, the tree in the window, the baby inside her. And the husband who wasn't home yet. "Doing fine."

He should have had the guy he hired find out more. He would have gotten some advance warning about that other man, about the baby coming. If he'd known, he wouldn't be here now, drinking vodka and looking like a fool.

"Your husband…" he said, and then didn't know how to go on.

She shook her head. "Marcus, I—"

"Stop." He tipped his glass at her. "On second thought, I really don't want to know." Another gulp and the second drink was finished. So was he. He set the glass down and stood. "I can see you're okay. That's good. You have a great life." He headed for the door.

"Marcus. Wait—"

But he wasn't listening. Four long strides and he reached the door.

As he yanked the door open, she called again, "Damn it, Marcus!" He shut the door behind him. Ignoring the sound of her calling after him, he made for the stairs, taking them two at a time, his throat tight and his chest aching.

In under a minute, he was across the central courtyard of her apartment complex, out the wrought-iron gate to the street and behind the wheel of his rented Lexus. He stuck the key in the ignition and turned it over. The engine purred.

But he didn't pull out into traffic. Instead, he flopped back in the seat and stared blindly at the dark windshield, seeing not the night beyond, but Hayley staring back at him through solemn eyes. Hayley, coming toward him with that second drink he'd demanded, her huge stomach leading the way.

She hadn't been wearing a wedding ring.

He sat up straighter. She'd quit her job as his assistant and left him in…May. Seven months ago.

In his mind's eye, he saw her answering the door again, her hand on her stomach. *Her beach-ball-size stomach.*

Marcus was no expert on pregnancy. But didn't she look further along than seven months? Really, she looked to him to be almost ready to have the kid…

His heart slammed into his breastbone and his stomach rolled as the world seemed to tip on its axis.

No ring on her ring finger. And the husband. He wasn't there because…

There *was* no husband.

Marcus yanked the key from the ignition and got out of the car. He raced across the sidewalk and up the three stone steps to the gate.

Which was locked.

He swore, a harsh oath, though there was no one but the night to hear him. Earlier, he'd lucked out and slipped in behind a couple too busy groping each other to notice they had company as they entered the complex. Not this time. He stood at the gate alone. Muttering another bad word, he punched the button that went with Hayley's apartment number.

She answered immediately, as if she'd been waiting by the receiver for him to finally add two and two and come up with four. "Marcus."

"Is it mine?"

By way of answer, she buzzed him in.

She was waiting in her open doorway when he reached the top of the stairs. Waiting in silence. No Christmas music now.

He asked, low, "Well?"

And she nodded. Slowly. Deliberately.

"And the husband?" he demanded. When she frowned as if puzzled, he clarified. "Is there a husband?"

Her head went back and forth. No husband.

He stared at her. He had absolutely zero idea what to do or say next.

She gestured for him to come in. Moving on autopilot, he reentered her apartment. She indicated the blue couch. So he went over there and lowered his strangely numb body onto the cushions again.

He watched as she reclaimed the blue chair,

those ringless pale hands of hers gripping the chair arms. His gaze was hopelessly drawn to her belly. He tried to get his mind around the bizarre reality that she had his baby in there.

His baby. His…

"Oh, Marcus," she said in a small voice at last. "I'm so—"

He cut her off by showing her the flat of his palm. "You *knew*, didn't you, when you left me? That's *why* you left me. Because of the baby."

She shook her head.

"What?" he demanded. "You're telling me you *didn't* know you were pregnant when you walked out on me?"

"I knew. All right? I knew." She pushed on the chair arms, as if she meant to rise. "Do we have to—?"

"Yeah. We do."

She sank back to the chair. "This is totally

unnecessary. Really. I'm not expecting anything of you."

"Just answer me. Did you leave me because you got pregnant?"

"Sort of."

"Damn it. Either you did, or you didn't."

She shut those shining eyes and sucked in a slow breath. When she looked at him again, she spoke with deliberate care. "I left because you didn't love me and you didn't want to marry me and you'd already told me, when we started in together, you made it so *perfectly* clear, that you would never get married again and you would never have children. I felt guilty, okay? For messing up and getting pregnant. But still, *I* wanted this baby. And that meant I couldn't see it as anything but a losing proposition to hang around in Seattle waiting for you to feel responsible for me and this child I'm having, even though you didn't want me and you don't want a kid. It was lose-lose, as far as I could see. So I came home."

Her tone really grated on him. As if she was so noble, just walking away, telling him nothing. As if, somehow, he was the one in the wrong here. "You should have told me before you walked out on me. I had a damn right to know."

Spots of color stained her pale cheeks. She straightened her shoulders. "Of course I planned to tell you."

"When?"

She glanced away. "It's…arranged."

"Arranged." He repeated the word. It made no sense to him. "Telling me I'm going to be a father is something you needed to *arrange?*"

She let go of the chair arms just long enough to throw up both hands. Then she slapped them down again. Hard. "Look. I was stressed over it, all right? I admit I didn't want to face you. But I have it set up so you would have known."

"You have it…set up?"

"Isn't that what I just said?"

"Set up for when?"

"As soon as the baby's born. You were going to know then."

"You were planning to…call me from the hospital?"

She swallowed. "Uh. Not exactly."

"Damn it, Hayley." He glared at her.

She curved a hand under her belly and snapped to her feet. "Come with me."

He stayed where he was and demanded, "Come where?"

"Just come with me. Please."

"Hayley…"

But she was already moving—and with surprising agility for someone so hugely pregnant. She zipped over and grabbed her bag, flung open the entry area closet and dragged a red wool coat from a hanger in there. She turned to him as she shrugged into the coat. “Where’s your car?”

“Out in front, but I don’t—”

“Are you drunk?”

“Drunk? What the hell? Of course I’m not drunk.”

“Okay.” She flipped her hair out from under the coat’s collar. “You can drive.”

He muttered a string of swearwords as he rose and followed her into the cold, mist-shrouded night.

Ten minutes later, she directed him to turn into the driveway of a green-shuttered white brick house on a quiet street lined with oaks and maples.

He pulled in where she pointed, stopped the car and took the key from the ignition. "Who lives here?"

"Come on," she said, as if that were any kind of answer. A moment later, she was up and out and headed around the front of the vehicle.

Against his own better judgment, he got out, too, and followed her up the curving walk to a red front door. She rang the bell.

As chimes sounded inside, he heard a dog barking and a child yelling, "I got it!"

The lock turned and the door flew open to reveal a brown-haired little girl in pink tights and ballet shoes. The dog, an ancient-looking black mutt about the size of a German shepherd, pawed the hardwood floor beside the girl and barked in a gravelly tone, "Woof," and then "woof," again, each sound produced with great effort.

"Quiet, Candy," said the child and the dog dropped to its haunches with a sound that could only be called a relieved sigh. The child beamed at Hayley and then shouted over her shoulder, "It's Aunt Hayley!"

Aunt Hayley? Impossible. To be an aunt, you needed a brother or a sister. Hayley had neither.

A woman appeared behind the child, a woman with softly curling brown hair and blue eyes, a woman who resembled Hayley in an indefinable way—something in the shape of the eyes, in the mouth that wasn't full, but had a certain teasing tilt at the corners. "Hey," the woman said, wiping her hands on a towel. "Surprise, surprise." She cast a questioning glance in Marcus's direction.

And Hayley said, "This is Marcus."

"Ah," said the woman, as if some major question had been answered. "Well. Come on in."

The kid and the old dog backed out of the way and Hayley and Marcus entered the warm, bright house. The woman led them through an open doorway into a homey-looking living room. Just as at Hayley's place, a lighted Christmas tree stood in the window, a bright spill of gifts beneath.

"Can I take your coats?" the woman asked. When Hayley shook her head, she added, "Well, have a seat, then."

Marcus hoped someone would tell him soon what the hell he was doing there. He dropped to the nearest wing chair as the kid launched herself into a pirouette. A bad one. She stumbled a little as she came around front again. And then she grinned, a grin as infectious as her mother's—and Hayley's.

"I'm DeDe." She bowed.

"Homework," said the mother.

"Oh, Mom…"

The mother folded her arms and waited, her kitchen towel trailing beneath her elbow.

Finally, the kid gave it up. "Okay, okay. I'm going," she grumbled. She seemed a cheerful type of kid and couldn't sustain the sulky act. A second later, with a jaunty wave in Marcus's direction, she bounced from the room, the old dog limping along behind her.

Hayley, who'd taken the other wing chair, said, "Marcus, this is my sister, Kelly."

It occurred to him about then that the evening was taking on the aspect of some bizarre dream: Hayley having his baby. The kid in the pink tights. The decrepit dog. The sudden appearance of a sister where there wasn't supposed to be one.

"A sister," he said, sounding as dazed as he felt. "You've got a sister…"

Hayley had grown up in foster homes. Her mother, who was frail and often sick, had trouble keeping a job and had always claimed she wasn't up to taking care of her *only* daughter. So she'd dumped Hayley into the system.

"Oh, Marcus." Hayley made a small, unhappy sound in her throat. "I realize this is a big surprise. It was to me, too. Believe me. My mother always told me I was the only one. It never occurred to me that she was lying, that anyone would lie about something like that…."

"Ah," said Marcus, hoping that very soon the surprises were going to stop.

The sister, Kelly, fingered her towel and smiled hopefully. "We have a brother, too…."

Hayley piped up again. "I just found them back in June—or rather, we all found each other. When Mom died."

His throat did something strange. He coughed into his hand to clear it. "Your mother died…."

"Yeah. Not long after I moved back here. I met Kelly and our brother, Tanner, in Mom's hospital room, as a matter of fact."

"When she was dying, you mean?"

"Yes. When she was dying." Before he could decide what to ask next, Hayley turned to her sister. "Could you get the letter, please?"

Kelly frowned. "Are you sure? Maybe you ought to—"

"Just get it."

"Of course." Kelly left the room.

Marcus sat in silence, staring at the woman who was soon to have his child. He didn't speak. And neither did she.

It was probably better that way.

The sister returned with a white envelope. She handed it to Hayley, who held it up so that he could see his own address printed neatly on the front. “Tell him, Kelly.”

Kelly sucked in a reluctant breath and turned to Marcus. “I would have mailed it to you, as soon as the baby was born.” She held up two balloon-shaped stickers, one pink, which said, It’s A Girl and the other blue, with It’s A Boy.

Hayley said weakly, “You know. Depending.”

Marcus looked at the envelope, at the long-lost sister standing there holding the stickers, at Hayley sitting opposite him, eyes wide, her hand resting protectively on her pregnant stomach.

I’m going to wake up, he thought. *Any second now, I’m going to wake up.*

But he didn’t.

Chapter Two

Hayley despised herself.

She'd blown this situation royally and she knew it. She stared at her baby's father in the chair across from hers and longed only to turn back time.

She should have told him. In hindsight, that much was achingly clear. She should have told him back in May, before she broke it off with him, before she quit her job as his assistant and slunk back to Sacramento to nurse her broken heart.

No matter his total rejection of her when she'd told him she loved him, he'd deserved to know. No matter that when she dared to suggest he might think again about them getting married, he'd given her a flat, unconditional no—and then, when she hinted they ought to break up, since they were clearly going nowhere, he'd agreed that was probably for the best.

No matter. None of it. She should have told him when she left him that he was going to be a dad. If she'd told him then, she wouldn't be looking across her sister's coffee table at him now, seeing the stunned bewilderment in his usually piercing green eyes, and totally hating herself.

She broke the grim silence that hovered like a gray cloud in her sister's living room. "Okay.

I messed up. I know it." She glanced down at the envelope. "This is no way to find out you're a dad. I can't believe I was going to do this. I…" She dared to glance up at him. Not moving. Was he even breathing? She pleaded, "Oh, Marcus. I wish you could understand. After how it ended with us, I just didn't know how to break it to you. This was the only way I could make sure I wouldn't chicken out and *never* get around to telling you."

Marcus stood.

She gulped. "Um. Are we going?"

"Oh, yeah. We're going."

Hayley slid the envelope into her purse as he turned and headed for the door. Without a backward glance, he went through the arch to the entrance hallway. She pushed herself upright as she heard the front door open—and then shut, a way-too-final sound.

Kelly sent her a look. "Oh, boy. He's mad."

"Maybe he'll just leave without me…." She almost wished that he would.

"I don't like this. You sure you're going to be okay with him?"

She gave her sister a game smile. "I'll be fine. Really."

Kelly stepped close and caught her hand. "Call me. If you need me…"

"I will. I promise."

"I'm here. You know that."

"I do. I'm glad…."

With a final, reassuring squeeze, Kelly released her.

Outside, Marcus was waiting behind the wheel with the engine running. He stared straight ahead. Hayley got in, stretched the seat belt long to fit over her tummy and hooked it.

Without once glancing in her direction, he backed from the driveway and off they went.

The short ride back to her place was awful. She tried not to squirm in her seat as she wondered if he'd ever look at her again—let alone actually speak.

At her apartment complex, he followed her wordlessly through the iron gate, across the central courtyard and up the steps to her door. She stuck her key in the lock and pushed the door wide.

He took her arm as she moved to enter. "The letter," he said.

"I…what?"

"Give me my letter."

"But there's nothing in it you don't know now and I don't see why—"

"You don't want me to read it." It was an accusation.

"I didn't say—"

"The letter," he repeated. He was looking at her now. Straight at her. She knew that look from two years of working for him, of falling hopelessly and ever-more-totally in love with him. When Marcus got that look, it meant he wouldn't stop until he had what he wanted. She might as well give in now. Because in the end, he would get the damn letter.

"All right," she said, as if she'd actually made a choice. She took the letter from her purse and handed it over.

He let go of her arm, but then instantly threatened, "Don't even imagine you can run away again."

She felt the angry heat as it flooded her cheeks. "What are you talking about? I left—you, my job and Seattle. I didn't *run away*. And I certainly am not going anywhere now.

This is my home. Especially now that I've found my family here."

"Just don't. Because I'll find you. You know I will."

She did know. But so what? She had zero intention of running off, so his point was totally moot. "I like it here," she insisted, hoping it might get through this time. "I'm going nowhere." She wrapped her arms around herself against the night chill and cast a longing glance toward the warmth and light beyond the threshold. "Are you coming in?"

"Not now," he replied, so imperious he set her teeth on edge. He spoke *at* her more than *to* her and he stared over her shoulder instead of meeting her eyes. She wondered as she'd wondered a thousand times, *why*, of all the men in all the world, had she gone and given her heart to Marcus Reid?

Probably her upbringing—or lack of one. Her mother had put her in the foster care system when she was a baby. And her father, the notorious kidnapper, murderer and serial husband, Blake Bravo? He'd been long gone by the time Hayley was born. Unavailable. That was the word for dear old dad. Unavailable in the most thorough sense of the word.

Which, she supposed, made it not the least surprising that she'd chosen an emotionally unavailable man to love.

"All right, then," she said. "Since you won't come in, good night." She started to turn toward the haven of her apartment.

But then he muttered distractedly, "I need to think. Then we'll talk."

She faced him once more. "That's fine with me." Though what, exactly, they would talk about was beyond her. What more was there to say? Not much. Not until after the baby was born, when they could discuss fun topics like custody and child support.

Oh, God. She dreaded all that. And she'd been avoiding facing what she dreaded.

Because she understood Marcus well enough to know that he'd never turn his back on his child. Even though he'd always insisted he didn't want children, now he was actually *having* one, everything would change. He was going to be *responsible* for a child. And Marcus Reid took his responsibilities with absolute seriousness.

He left at last. She went inside and shut the door and ordered her pulse to stop racing, her heart to stop bouncing around under her breastbone.

Marcus knew her secret now. Getting all worked up over the situation wasn't going to make him go away.

Chapter Three

Marcus,

I don't know where to start. So I guess I'll just put it right out there. If you're reading this it's because you're a father. I've just had your baby and this letter has been mailed to you because the baby is born and doing fine. The sticker on the envelope should tell you whether it's a boy or a girl.

I'm so sorry. I know you're furious with me about now. I don't blame you. I should

have told you before I left Seattle, but…
well, I just couldn't make myself do it.

So you're learning this way. In a letter.

Try not to hate me too much.

Try not to hate me too much….

Marcus read that sentence over twice. And then a third time.

After that, he loosened his tie. Then he dropped back across the hotel room bed and stared at the attractively coffered ceiling and thought how she was wrong: he didn't hate her. True, what he felt for Hayley right then wasn't pretty. It was fury and frustration and a certain wounded possessiveness all mixed up together.

But hate? Uh-uh. He wished he did hate her. It would make everything so much simpler.

He raised the letter and read the rest. She'd

listed the address and phone number of the hospital she would be using. And also the information he already had—her own address and number.

She wrote at the bottom:

Try to understand. I realize this isn't what you wanted. I swear I was careful. I guess just not careful enough.
Hayley

That was it. All of it. It wasn't much more information than he'd already had.

He balled up the letter, raised his arm and tossed the thing into the corner wastebasket. Slam dunk.

What the hell to do now?

He was due back in Seattle tomorrow, for a series of meetings, the first of which he had on his schedule for 11:00 a.m. His company was poised for a big move into the Central California market. They were high priority, those meetings.

But then again, so was the kid he'd just found out he was having.

And so was Hayley. She needed him now, whether her pride would let her admit that or not.

Still flat on his back across the bed, he grabbed his PDA off the nightstand and dialed—with his thumb, from memory. She answered on the second ring.

"'Lo?" Her voice was husky, reminding him of other nights, of the scent and the feel of her, all soft and drowsy, in his bed.

"You were already asleep." He didn't mean it to come out sounding like an accusation, but he supposed that it did.

"Marcus." She sighed. "What?"

"I'm flying out at 6:00 a.m. tomorrow. I've got meetings in Seattle I can't get out of."

"You've always got meetings you can't get out of. It's fine. I told you. I don't expect—"

"I'll clear my calendar in the next couple of days. Then I'll come back."

"You don't have to do that."

"Yeah. I do. We both know I do. I'll see you. Thursday. Friday at the latest. If you need me before then, call me on my cell. You still have the number?"

A silence, then, "I have it."

"When's the baby due?"

"January eighth."

"You're not working, are you?" He heard rustling, pictured her sitting up in bed, all rumpled and droopy-eyed, her hair tangled from sleep. "Hayley?"

Reluctantly, she answered, “Yes. I’m still working.”

“You shouldn’t be. And now you’ve finally told me about the baby, you don’t need to be. I’ll make arrangements right away.”

“Give me money, you mean.” She sounded downright bleak. She’d damn well better not try refusing his money. “I’m managing just fine. I like working and I feel great and I’m going to stay on the job until—”

“Quit. Tomorrow.”

“Uh. Excuse me. But this is *my* life you’re suddenly running. Don’t.”

“I’m only saying—”

“Don’t.”

He had no idea where she worked, or what she did there. His own fault. He’d just *had* to play it noble seven months ago, which meant only allowing the detective to get the basic information.

So that now he was forced to ask, “Where do you work, anyway?”

“I’m an office manager. For a small catering company. There’s the owner, the chef, the dishwasher and me. We’re in a storefront off of K Street. Around the Corner Catering. We do a pretty brisk business, actually. We’re hooked up with a staffing agency so we offer full service. Not only the food, but the staff, from setup to cleanup.”

“A caterer. You work for a caterer.”

“Yeah. Is that a problem for you?”

“It’s high-stress work and you know it. Chefs are notorious for being temperamental. You’re having a baby. You shouldn’t be in a stressful work environment. You should—”

“Don’t,” she said for the third time.

He let it go. Later, when he got back, they could discuss this again. He’d get her to see this his way—the *right* way. "I'll be gone two days. Three at the most."

"You said that."

"No, I said I'd be back Thursday or Friday. On second thought, I should be able to make it sooner. Wednesday, I hope."

"All right. Wednesday, then. Is that all?"

He hated to hang up with all this…tension between them. He should say something tender, he supposed. But nothing tender occurred to him. "We'll work this out. You can count on me."

"I know that."

"Don't worry."

"I…won't," she said softly after a moment. Then, almost in a whisper, "Good night, Marcus." Then a click.

He put the device back on the night table and laced his hands behind his head. A kid. It still didn't seem possible. A child had never been part of his plans.

But plans changed. And sometimes allowances had to be made.

"His assistant called me at work an hour ago," Hayley told Kelly when the sisters met for lunch the next day. "Her name is Joyce. She sounds very…efficient."

"That's good, right?" Kelly forked up a bite of Caesar salad.

Hayley turned her glass of Perrier in a slow circle. "I mean, not young, you know?"

Kelly swallowed and frowned, puzzled. "Not young…like you?"

Hayley turned her glass some more. "It shouldn't matter, that he hired someone older to replace me."

"But you're glad he did."

Hayley tried to deny it—and couldn't. "I suppose I am. Even though, since I left, he's been going out with a bunch of beautiful women."

"Oh, really?"

"Oh, yeah."

"How do you know that?"

"I still get *Seattle* magazine. I saw a picture of him in a tux." She gazed wistfully down into her überpricey glass of bubbly French water. "He looks amazing in a tux. It was some opening of something. He had a drop-dead gorgeous blonde on his arm. He looked so…severe. And dangerous. And handsome—did I mention handsome?"

"Often."

"Practically broke my poor little heart all over again."

"Jerk."

"No. He's not a jerk. He's…just Marcus, that's all. He was true to me when we were together. As a matter of fact, he's not real big on the bachelor lifestyle. But then, when we broke up, well, he would have considered it a point of honor, to prove to himself that he was over me."

Kelly shook her head. "Did I already say the word *jerk?*"

"You did. And I said he's not. He's just… well, you'd have to know him."

Her sister wisely withheld comment. They ate in silence for a few minutes. Finally, Kelly spoke. "So the two of you got together…?"

"Six months after he hired me, when his divorce became final."

"He was married?"

"To his childhood sweetheart. But she

dumped him and ran off with some European guy. I was just burning hot for him. And I was lying in wait for those final divorce papers to come in the mail. Then I seduced him. It's a plain, shameless fact."

Kelly chuckled, "My bad baby sister."

"Oh, yeah. I was so sure I could show him what real, true love could be." Hayley shook her head. "So much for that." She bit into her grilled chipotle chicken sandwich and chewed slowly. The last month or two, with the baby taking up so much space in there, eating fast meant heartburn later.

"So what did his new, *older* assistant have to say?" Kelly buttered a sourdough roll.

"She was just telling me a platinum card was on the way, wanting to know where I banked so she could arrange for a giant-sized wire transfer of funds."

"Money," Kelly said thoughtfully. "Well, it comes in handy, you gotta admit."

"It sure does. I suppose I should be more grateful, huh?"

Kelly chuckled. "Oh, hell no. *He* should be grateful, to have a beautiful, smart, capable, loving woman like you as the mother of his child."

"I'll tell him you said that."

"Do."

"He's just a little messed over, that's all. From the awful childhood he had, from his marriage that didn't last forever, after all. I should embroider myself a sampler and hang it on the wall…."

"Saying?"

"'There's no saving a messed-over guy, so you're better off not to even try.'" Hayley chuckled, a sound devoid of humor. "Hey. It rhymes."

"Pure poetry."

"Kelly?"

"Umm?"

"Do you think *I'm* messed over? You know, from the way I grew up?"

Kelly shrugged. "Maybe a little. But we all are, I'm sure. You, me, big brother Tanner—and all the other poor, lost souls who had crazy, bad Blake Bravo for a dad. Think about it." Blake had married a lot of women. *And* given them children. Each woman had thought she was the only one. And they all found out much later, after the notorious Blake finally died and it was all over the national news, that there were other wives. Several. Some no doubt were yet to be found—along with the children they'd borne him. "None of us ever knew our father," Kelly continued, "even the ones who saw him now and then. Because he wasn't the kind that anybody really knows. And then, we all had mothers with emotional issues. That's a given. Remember Mom."

"God. Mom. Yeah." Lia Wells Bravo had been frail both physically and emotionally, the perfect target for Blake Bravo's dangerous brand of charm. One by one, she put the children he gave her during his infrequent visits into foster homes. Lia told all three they had no siblings. And though she wouldn't take care of them herself, she refused to give them up for adoption.

"It's just a sad fact," Kelly said. "Anybody who'd fall in love with a man like Blake Bravo would have had to be at least a little bit out of her mind."

"You're not exactly reassuring me, you know." Hayley sipped her Perrier.

"Sorry…"

"It's so depressing, just thinking about Mom. I hate that I never understood her. And now she's gone, I probably never will." She looked down at her sandwich and knew she ought to eat more of it. "Did I mention that Marcus's childhood was terrible, too?"

"You did. Have you met his parents?"

"They're both long dead. His mother died when he was a kid, some kind of accident. Marcus was never really clear on what happened to her, exactly. His father was a drunk and Marcus despised him. He got millions when his dad died. Marcus put it all away, hasn't touched a penny of it. He has it set up so it funds a bunch of charities. The whole Kaffe Central thing? He built that himself. Starting from a corner coffee shop in Tacoma where he went to work as a manager straight out of college."

"Kaffe Central. You said it's like Starbucks, right?"

Hayley leaned across the table. "Never," she commanded darkly, "compare the Kaffe Central experience to Starbucks." And then she grinned. "But, yeah. Helpful, skilled baristas. Quality coffee. Lattes to die for, whipped up just the way you want them. Amazing ambience—special, but…comfortable. Selected bakery treats."

"Wi-Fi?"

"As a matter of course. Oh, and it's a progressive company, too. Good working conditions, good salaries, everybody gets stock options, good benefits including health insurance. And from what Marcus said, you'll have one in your neighborhood soon. They're opening several shops here in the Sacramento area."

"Can't wait—and he sounds…like a complex man."

"He is. And determined. Way determined. Now he knows about the baby, he's going to be pushing me to do things his way. And I mean *every*thing."

"Marriage?"

Hayley laughed. "Are you kidding? After what his ex, Adriana, did to him, Marcus has sworn he'll never get married again."

"But now that he's going to be a dad…"

"Not Marcus. No way, not even with a baby coming. He may push for full custody, though."

Kelly scoffed. "But I thought you said he didn't even *want* kids."

"He didn't. But now it's happening, it's all going to be about doing the right thing, whatever he decides the right thing may be. He can be… cold. Distant. There's an emotional disconnect there that can be way scary. But he does have an ingrained sense of fair play. So my guess is he'll probably be willing to share custody."

"Big of him."

"But he'll want me to move back to Seattle, you watch. And he's already been on me to quit work immediately."

"Don't let him scare you. We can sic Tanner on him." Their older brother was a private investigator. Strong. Silent. Smart. Possibly as determined as Marcus. And extremely protective of his sisters and his niece.

"Even Tanner isn't going to be able to keep Marcus Reid from doing it all *his* way."

"But *you* will," said Kelly. "You're tough and smart, Hayley Bravo. Nobody pushes you around. You survived our poor, screwed-up mom *and* the foster care system with a positive attitude and a heck of a lot of heart. You're going to be just fine—and your baby, too."

"Say that again."

"It'll work out. You'll see."

Hayley took another bite of her sandwich and fervently hoped that her sister was right.

She found Marcus sitting in one of the wicker chairs by her front door when she got home from work that night. He wore a pricey gray trench over a beautiful charcoal suit and he looked as if he'd just stepped off the cover of *GQ*.

She met those ice-green eyes and felt an unwilling thrill skate along the surface of her skin. In spite of everything—her stomach out to here, her wounded heart, and the threat he posed to the destiny of her child—the man could steal her breath away with just a look.

"It's after six," he muttered, those eyes of his looking dangerous and shadowed, the Christmas lights that twined the railing casting his sculpted cheekbones into rugged relief. "What kind of hours are you working, anyway?"

"Nice to see you, too." She unlocked the front door and pushed it inward, then stepped back to gesture him in ahead of her.

He rose with a certain manly, regal grace that made her want to do sexy things to his tall, lean body, things she *shouldn't* want to do to him after the way he'd turned her down months ago—things she probably *couldn't* do in her current condition.

"Are you all right?" He was scowling. "I don't like it. You on your feet all day with the baby coming any minute now."

"I'm not due for almost a month. And I'm hardly working on my feet. I'm at a desk, thank you very much. Tonight, we had two events—a cocktail thing and a small dinner party—on the schedule, so I stayed a little late to give a hand with the last-minute details." As usual, there had been yelling on the part of the chef, Federico. Sofia, the owner, had yelled back. And it all came together beautifully in the end, just as it always did.

"Caterers," he grumbled. "I know how they are. Damn temperamental. Lots of shouting, everything a big drama." Okay, so he had Sofia—and Federico—nailed. No way she was copping to it. "It can't be good for the baby, for you to be in a stressful environment like that."

"You're repeating yourself."

"This issue bears repeating."

"It's not good for the baby if I get pneumonia, either." She pulled her coat a little closer against the evening chill. "But still, you seem determined to keep me standing out here all night."

He said something under his breath—something unpleasant, she had no doubt—and then, at last, he acquiesced to enter her apartment. Close on his heels, she turned on the light and shut the door.

They faced each other across the cramped entry area.

"You're back early…." She forced a smile, feeling suddenly strange about all this: the two of them, the baby, all the ways he'd denied her seven months ago, the secret she'd kept that she had no right to keep, a secret as pointless as it was wrong.

Because, in the end, here he was again. Back in her life. Determined to look after her and the baby whether they needed looking after or not.

"I took a few days off," he said with a scowl.

"You never take days off."

"First time for everything."

"I thought you had…meetings."

"I did. I made them quick. I cleared my

calendar. For tomorrow and the next day." His eyes held a flinty gleam and the determined set to that sensual slash of a mouth told her that he had plans. Plans concerning her and the baby and their future. Plans that he would implement within the next forty-eight hours—whether she liked them or not.

Hayley kept her smile in place. "Your coat?" He shrugged out of it. She hung it up, along with her own. "A drink?"

"No. Thanks."

Seeking a little good cheer—as well as an excuse to put some distance between them—she went to the tree. Dropping to an awkward crouch, she plugged it in. The Christmas lights came on, so happy and bright. Festive.

In all the years of her lonely childhood, there had always been a tree: in the group home, where she went between families. And in the various foster homes. And there was always at least one gift for her under each of those trees. So that she'd come to think of Christmas as something special, something magical and glowing in an otherwise drab life lived out in a series of other people's houses. Christmas was colorful, and optimistic, with joyous music that brought a fond tear to her eye.

Funny, but Kelly said she felt just the same way about the holidays….

"Come on." Marcus was there, standing above her. He held down a hand. She put hers in it, shocked at how good it felt—to touch his long, strong fingers again….

Oh, she would have to watch herself. She was just a big sucker when it came to this man.

He pulled her heavy body upward and she let him, leaning into him a little—but not too much. And as soon as she was upright, she stepped back, away from the delicious temptation to press herself and their baby against him, to find out if he would put those lean arms around her, if he'd cradle her close and put his lips to her hair.

She asked, "Have you eaten?"

"It's not necessary for you to—"

"Not the question. Did you have dinner?"

"No."

"I made spaghetti last night, before you… dropped in. There's plenty left. I'll just heat it up and do the salad. Have a seat. The remote's right there on the arm of the couch. Watch the news. It won't take long…."

He stared at her for several seconds. She wondered what he might be thinking. Finally, with a shrug, he went over to the couch and sat down.

A short time later, she called him to the

kitchen. He turned off the news and came to join her at her tiny table. They ate mostly in silence. She found her small appetite had fled completely. Dread was taking up what little space there was in her stomach. Still, she forced herself to put the food in her mouth, to slowly chew, to grimly swallow. The baby needed dinner. And really, so did she.

When they were through, Marcus got up and cleared the table while she loaded the dishwasher and wiped the counters. Then they went to the living room. He took a chair and she sat on the couch.

Her pulse, she realized as she sank into the cushions, had sped into overdrive. Her palms had gone clammy. And her stomach was aching, all twisted with tension. The baby kicked. She winced and put her hand over the spot.

"Are you sick?" He frowned at her.

She shook her head. "Just…dreading this conversation."

"You're too pale."

"I'm a redhead. My skin is naturally pale."

"Paler than usual, I mean."

"Can we just get on with it? Please? Tell me what you want and we can…take it from there."

"I *don't* want to upset you."

She folded her hands over her stomach. "I'm fine." It was a lie. But a necessary one. "Just tell me what you have in mind. Just say it."

"Hayley, I think…" The words trailed off. He looked at her through brooding eyes.

"What? You think, what?" She fired the question at him twice—and as she did, somehow, impossibly, she *knew* what he was going to tell her, what he was going to want from her. It was the one thing she'd been beyond-a-doubt certain he *wouldn't* be pushing for.

But he was. He did. "I think we should get married. All things considered, now there's a kid involved, I think it's the best way to go here."

Married. The impossible word seemed to hover in the air between them.

Now that there was a baby, he wanted to marry her....

She unfolded her hands and lifted them off her stomach and then didn't know what to do with them. She looked down at them as if they belonged on someone else's body. "Married," she said back to him, still not quite believing.

"Yes." He gave a single nod. "Married."

She braced her hands on the sofa cushions and dared to remind him, "But you don't want to be married again. Ever. You know you don't. You *told* me you don't."

Did he wince? She could have sworn he did.

"It's the best way," he said again, as if that made it totally acceptable—for him to do exactly what he'd promised he would never do.

Okay, now. The awful thing? The really pitiful thing?

Her heart leaped.

It did. It jumped in her chest and did the happy dance. Because marrying Marcus? That was her dearest, most fondly held dream.

From the moment she'd met him—that rainy Monday, two months out of Heald's Business College and brand-new to Seattle, when he interviewed her for the plum job of his executive assistant—she'd known she would love him. Known that he, with his piercing, watchful eyes and sexy mouth, his wary heart that was kinder than he wanted it to be, his dry sense of humor so rarely seen…

He was her love. He was the one she had

been waiting for, dreaming of, through all her lonely years until that moment.

Marriage to Marcus. Oh, yeah. It was what she'd longed for, what she'd hoped against hope might happen someday.

Because she loved him. She'd known from the first that she would. And within weeks of going to work for him, she was his. Completely, without reservation, though he refused to touch her for months.

She waited. She schemed.

And then his divorce became final. She went to his house wearing a yellow raincoat, high heels, a few wisps of lingerie and nothing else.

At last, they were lovers. No, he didn't love her. Oh, but she loved him.

God help her, she sometimes feared that she would *always* love him. And her love…it was like Christmas to her. It was magic. And bright colored lights. It was that one present with her name on it under a new foster mother's tree.

"Hayley?" His voice came to her. The voice of her beloved. Dreamed of. Yearned after—and yet, in the end, no more hers than all the foster families she'd grown up with.

She pressed her lips together, shook her head, stared bleakly past him, at the shining lights of her tree.

"Damn it, Hayley. What do you want from me? You want me to beg you? I'm willing. Anything. Just marry me and let me take care of you. And our baby. Let me—"

"Stop." The sound scraped itself free of her throat.

He swore. A word harsh and graphic. But at least after that, he fell silent.

She met his eyes. "What if there was no baby, if I wasn't pregnant…?"

"But you are."

"Work with me here. *If* I wasn't. Would you be asking me to marry you now?"

A muscle danced in his jaw. "I would, yes. I love you."

The lie was so huge, she almost smiled. And the knot that was her stomach had eased a little. She felt better now. She knew she could hold out against him, against her impossible dream that he would someday find his way to her, that at last he would see she was the only one for him.

But he hadn't found his way to her, not in his secret heart. And he never would.

"Marcus. Come on. You're lying."

"No. I'm not."

"Please. This is not going to work."

"The hell it won't. I came here to see you, didn't I, showed up at your door last night? And I had no damn clue about the baby then."

Okay. Point for him. But hardly a winning one.

She challenged, "You're telling me you came here because you realized you couldn't live without me?"

"That's right."

"You didn't want to go another day without me at your side? You came here intending to ask me to marry you, after all, to beg me to give our love another chance and be your bride at last, to make you the happiest man on earth, make all your dreams come true?"

He looked at her steadily. It was not a pleasant look. "Damn you, Hayley. I want to marry you *now*. Why does it matter what I would have done if you hadn't been pregnant?"

"Is that a real question?"

"Excuse me?"

"Do you really want to know why it matters?"

"Yes. I do."

"All right. It matters because in all my life, except for the sister and brother I found in June at my mother's deathbed, I've never had anyone to really call my own. I've worn other people's hand-me-downs, lived in other people's houses, been the extra kid, the one who didn't really belong. The one who never had a home of her own."

"I'm offering you—"

"Wait. I'm not finished. What I'm trying to say is that I had no choice, about the way I grew up. But I do have a choice now. When I get married, I'm going to finally *belong* to someone. Completely. Lovingly. Openly. And the man I marry will belong to *me*."

"I *will* belong to you. I'll be true to you, I'll never betray you."

"Well, of course you wouldn't. You're not the kind to cheat. Except in your secret heart."

"That's not so."

"It is. You know it is. You'll never belong to me, Marcus. You belong to Adriana. You always have and you always will."

Chapter Four

Marcus regarded the pregnant woman on the blue couch. At least she had a little color in her cheeks now. Telling him all the nonsensical reasons she wouldn't have him as a husband had brought a warm flush to her velvety skin.

Terrific. She had pink cheeks and he wanted to…

Hell. He didn't know what he wanted to do, exactly. Something violent. Something loud.

Something to snap her out of this silly resistance she was giving him and make it crystal clear to her that she was making no damn sense and she ought to smarten up and get with the program.

Adriana wasn't the issue here. She'd walked away, divorced him. That part of his life was over. For good.

Hayley loved him and needed him. He was willing, at last, to be what she needed.

He spoke, the soul of reason. "I'm here, now, today, and ready to do what you wanted. You left me because I wouldn't marry you. And now I *want* to marry you. I want to give you exactly what you were asking for all along. I don't understand why you have to be difficult about this. You're not behaving rationally. And one of your finest qualities has always been your ability to step back and assess a situation logically. I advise you to do that. Now."

"Marcus."

He hated when she said his name like that. So patiently. As if he were a not-very-bright oversize child. It was supremely annoying, the way she got to him, the way he *let* her get to him. He'd graduated from Stanford at the top of his class; he'd built a billion-dollar corporation from virtually nothing. He knew how to deal with people, how to get along and get what he wanted.

But with Hayley, somehow, since she'd decided she loved him and wanted to marry him, he hadn't known how to deal at all. First, she left him because he *wouldn't* marry her. And now that he said he *would* marry her, she was turning him down.

And she was talking again. All patience and

gentleness, trying to make him understand. "No. You don't *want* to marry me. You want to take care of your child—and the mother of your child. You think marrying me is the best way to do that, to take care of us. I admire you for that. I truly do. You are a fine man and I'm proud to be having your baby. But that kind of marriage—marriage you want because it's the *right* thing? Uh-uh. That's just not what *I* want. And it's not what our baby needs, either. Our baby needs—no. Our baby *deserves* a loving home, a *happy* home. How can our baby have that if you're resentful because you felt you had to marry me?"

"Whoa." He waited, just to be sure she was going to stop talking and listen for a moment. When she stayed quiet, he said slowly and clearly, "Don't characterize me. Please. I'm not resentful. Not in the least. And you know me well enough by now to know that I never do anything because I have to. I never do anything I don't *want* to do."

She was shaking her head. "All right. Have it your way. You want to marry me. Because you feel that you *have* to."

He stood. "Hayley."

She gazed up at him, her expression angelic. "What?"

"I'm going to go now." *Before my head explodes.*

"Oh, Marcus…"

He went to the closet by the door and got his coat. "We can…work this out tomorrow." He'd regroup, come at this problem in a fresh, new way—true, at this point he hadn't a clue what that way might be. But something would come to him, some way to get through to her, to make her see reason.

"There's nothing to work out," she said brightly. "Not when it comes to marriage, anyway—and where are you staying?"

He named his hotel. "Tomorrow, then."

She was on her feet, her hands pressed together as if in prayer, her expression verging on tender, her eyes at that moment sea-blue. He wanted to cover the distance between them, sweep her into his arms and taste those lips he'd been missing for so many months.

But no. Later for kissing. After she realized he was right about this. After she agreed to marry him and come home with him where he could take care of her, where she—and their baby—belonged.

In his hotel suite, Marcus checked his messages. There were several, each representing a different potential disaster. He made a string of calls to his associates. They brainstormed and came up with the necessary steps to eradicate the issues before they became catastrophes. By the time he hung up from the final call of the night, he was reassured that things in Seattle were as under control as they were likely to get until he could handle this situation with Hayley and return to work.

Next, he checked his e-mail, one eye on CNN as he made his replies, keeping a couple of IM conversations going at the same time, taking two more calls and answering questions as he worked. At last, with the phone quiet and the replies made, he put on his gym clothes and went down to the guest gym to work out.

Aside from the night before, when he had learned about the baby, Marcus never touched liquor—or drugs of any kind. His father had been a hopeless and violent drunk and Marcus was determined, above all, not to follow in the old man's footsteps. But his high-stress lifestyle demanded he find some way to relax and blow off steam. So he worked out.

An hour and a half later, dripping sweat, his legs and arms rubbery from pushing every muscle to the limit, he returned to his rooms and hit the shower. It was after one when he went to bed. By then he'd decided on his next move with Hayley and his confidence had returned.

Tomorrow, she would see things his way and agree to be his wife. They could be married in Nevada ASAP. And then she could return to Seattle with him and take it easy until the baby was born. They would have a good life, a full life.

He'd long ago accepted that he would never be a father. But now that it was happening, he was realizing he really didn't mind at all.

* * *

At seven the next morning, when Hayley opened the blinds on the living room window, she saw Marcus sitting out there on her balcony next to the miniature tree. She was tempted, just for the sake of being contrary, to let him sit there.

But it was cold out. Even from the far side of the window, with him facing away from her toward the central courtyard, she could see the way his breath plumed in the air.

It just wouldn't be right, to let her baby's father freeze to death on her landing.

She went and opened the door. At the sound, he turned and looked at her. Once again, she was forced to ignore the shiver of pleasure that skittered through her, just from meeting those watchful green eyes.

"I thought you'd never get up."

She gathered her robe a little closer around her and spoke in a tone meant to show he didn't thrill her in the least. "How do you keep slipping through the security gate, that's what I'd like to know?"

His fine mouth hinted at a wry smile as he stood. "Nobody keeps me out when I'm determined to get in." His eyes said he was talking about more than a locked gate. Another shiver. She told herself it was the cold. "Make me some coffee?"

She couldn't help teasing him, "You know, there's a Starbucks just two blocks away on—"

"Very funny." He asked again—or rather demanded, "Coffee. I need coffee."

"Oh, all right."

He followed her in, put his coat in the closet, then sat at the table and got out his PDA as she ground the beans and got the pot started. He poked at the tiny keys a mile a minute while she heated the water for her own special pregnant-lady herbal tea blend.

"I'm having oatmeal," she told him. "Want some?"

He glanced up from the device in his hand. "Sounds good. Thanks." She got to work on the oatmeal as he finished on the BlackBerry and put it away. "Can I help?"

"Why not? Bowls are in there." She indicated a cabinet. "Mugs there." She pointed again. "Spoons in here." She pulled out a drawer.

He rose and washed his hands and then set the table. It was…nice, she thought. Peaceful and domestic, the two of them in her little apartment, putting the simple breakfast together.

Not that she was changing her mind about anything. She wasn't. Though she had no doubt he would be putting the pressure on again any minute now.

She was right.

She sat down to her bowl of oats and reached for the brown sugar. A ring waited behind it. A truly amazing ring. The enormous central diamond winking at her in the early-morning light.

The thing was gorgeous. The main stone had to be four carats, maybe five, Marquise cut—wasn't that what they called that near-oval shape that tapered to a point at either end? A matched pair of gorgeous round diamonds snuggled up close on either side. The setting? Platinum. Of course.

It was...*more*, that ring. More than she would have chosen. More than she had dared to imagine, more than she ever could have hoped for, back in the day when she allowed herself the luxury of fantasizing about such things as engagement rings.

It was showy and perfect and it probably cost more than her yearly salary at Around the Corner Catering. She just ached to grab it and try it on—and never take it off. Even with her finger puffy from pregnancy, she knew it would fit….

And Marcus was watching her. "I meant to give it to you last night. But you were so busy saying no, I never got the chance."

"It's absolutely beautiful."

"I'm glad you like it."

"But I can't accept it, and you know I can't."

He sipped his coffee. "I thought we could go to Las Vegas. We could be married this afternoon."

She repeated, gently, with honest regret, "I'm not going to marry you. I told you that."

He didn't say a word, only looked at her, eyes level. Zero emotion. It was one of those moments where you could have heard a feather stir the air as it drifted to the floor.

Finally, he set down his mug, took out a velvet box and put the ring inside. He snapped the box closed and slipped it into a pocket. "You through with that brown sugar?"

She spooned some on her cereal and passed it to him. Same with the milk. She took some; so did he.

He tried it. "Good."

She nodded, longing to insist that she really did love the ring. She did appreciate his effort—or his nice older-lady assistant's effort, which was probably more likely. No way he'd managed to clear his calendar and get back here in one day and *still* have time to choose a ring. Whatever. It didn't matter who chose the ring. She *was* touched and she did want him to know that.

But going on about how touched she was would only increase his confidence that he was making progress toward getting her to marry him. Uh-uh. Wedding bells were not going to be ringing for them and the sooner he accepted that, the better.

He asked, "What time are you due at work?"

"Nine."

"And you're there until six?"

"No. Unless something comes up unexpectedly, we have no parties scheduled for tonight. I should be done by two or three." She felt just bad enough about the ring to volunteer more details. "I'm training my replacement. My last day is a week from Friday, as a matter of fact."

His expression didn't change. "I'll drive you."

"Uh. To work?"

"Yes."

"Really. That's not—"

"Humor me, all right? I'll drive you there and pick you up when you're finished."

"But I don't…" She let the refusal fade off into nothing. She knew by his carved-in-stone expression that he wasn't backing down on this. Not without a fight. And right then, after getting a look at that beautiful ring she couldn't accept, she just didn't have the heart to hold the line that hard with him. "All right. A ride is great. Thanks."

Around the Corner Catering had space in a new-looking strip mall. A brick facade and lots of windows, with well-tended flower beds out front.

Not bad, Marcus thought. In an upscale commercial area. At least she wasn't working in a rough part of town.

Hayley asked him to drive around back, where she pointed at a steel door bearing a plaque that read Around the Corner. "That's it."

Marcus nosed the car into an empty space opposite the door.

She sent him an apprehensive glance. "I'm not sure exactly what time I'll be finished...."

"Call when you're ready. You have the number?"

"I do, thanks." She got out and started for the building. He waited until she disappeared through the door before he backed and drove away.

The morning had been pretty much a loss. He'd gotten nowhere with her. And given that he damn well wasn't leaving until she agreed to leave with him, he was stuck another day in Sacramento.

Hell. He'd been so certain the ring was going to do it. Women went nuts for a big, fat diamond.

Most women, anyway. Not Hayley, though. At least not nuts enough to stop being so damn stubborn and let him do right by her.

Maybe he hadn't been romantic enough. He wasn't much good at the romantic stuff, never had been. Adriana used to complain about that all the time—how he wouldn't know a romantic gesture if it hit him on the head.

Marcus accepted his limitations in that area. He'd always thought that Hayley did, too. When things were good between them, she'd sworn she loved him just the way he was.

"You're not the least romantic," she'd told him once. They were in bed. After an amazing

hour of lovemaking. *"But you are sexy as hell, Marcus Reid. Never change...."*

He didn't intend to change. Still, hiding that big rock behind the brown sugar had been kind of cute. And the expression on her face when she saw it waiting there...

Priceless.

But he probably should have dropped to his knees the minute she spotted it and spouted something tender and poetic about how much she meant to him, about how he couldn't live another nanosecond without her at his side.

If he'd planned ahead better, he could have copped some flowery phrases off the Internet, been prepared to rattle them off at just the right moment.

Seeing him on his knees, spouting love poems. Now, that would have shocked her. Enough to get her to say yes?

He'd never know now. The opportunity was blown.

He headed for his hotel and a couple of hours on the phone, conferencing with his managers, getting them up to speed on how they would be handling things on their own for yet another twenty-four hours.

By noon, he felt he had everything on track—or at least as on track as it was going to get until he could take the reins in person again. That left him a couple of hours to kill before he picked up Hayley.

He knew just how to make the best use of that time: the brother.

In a situation as sticky as this one was turning out to be, Marcus could use an ally. Someone to support his case with Hayley. He'd considered approaching the sister, trying to get her on his side. But having seen Kelly with Hayley Monday night, he didn't foresee much assistance coming from that angle. Whatever choice Hayley made, Kelly would back her up.

Even if it was the *wrong* choice. Kelly wouldn't presume to tell her sister what she ought to do unless Hayley asked for her advice.

A brother, on the other hand, might damn well presume. A brother might push for his sister to do what was right, even if he had to stick his nose in where it didn't strictly belong.

Tuesday, between meetings, Marcus had contacted that P.I. again—the one he'd hired months ago to find out where Hayley had gone. This time he'd asked for a full report.

Within hours, the P.I. got back to him with basic information about Kelly and Tanner Bravo. Things like addresses and phone numbers, where they worked and their marital status.

Neither was married. Or ever had been. Kelly was the director of a family shelter. And Tanner owned and operated his own P.I. firm, Dark Horse Investigations.

Marcus went to Tanner's office in Rancho Cordova without calling first—and got nowhere. The office, in an undistinguished two-story building, was locked. No one answered his knock.

So much for the advantage of the face-to-face approach. He called the number his own investigator had given him and left his name and cell number. Tanner returned his call within minutes.

Marcus said, "I'm the father of Hayley's baby. I'd like to meet with you. Now, if possible."

Tanner Bravo had one question—the right one. "Where?"

"My hotel." He gave the name and the address. "The bar off the lobby."

"Half an hour?"

"I'll be there."

Marcus was nursing a club soda at the bar, text messaging his assistant, when Tanner appeared. Dark-haired and dark-eyed, he bore only a faint resemblance to his sisters.

"You're Reid," he said. "My sister's former boss." It wasn't a question. And he didn't offer to shake hands.

Marcus grabbed his drink. "Let's get a table."

They moved to a deuce in a shadowed corner. A cocktail waitress approached.

Tanner put a ten on the table. "Water. Ice."

She trotted off and returned in under a minute.

Marcus said, "That's all." And she left them.

Tanner glanced at his glass, but didn't bother to pick it up. He gave Marcus a dark look. "Welcome to Sacramento."

"Thanks. You should know I'm here to marry your sister."

The other man considered for a moment. In the end, he nodded. "Well. Good to know."

"She failed to mention the baby when she left me seven months ago. If she had, we'd be married now."

"And you wanted to meet with me because…?"

"I want to…get to know her family."

Tanner simply sat there. Marcus knew he was waiting for him to get to the point.

Might as well go for it. "She says she loves me. I've asked her several times in the past couple of days to marry me. But she refuses."

"Why?"

Marcus didn't want to go into how Hayley was so damn sure he didn't love her because of Adriana. So he gave the other man a partial answer. “Hayley thinks I’ll resent her for *forcing* me into it.”

“Will you?”

“Resent her? Hell, no. It’s the best thing. I can take care of her and I want to take care of her.”

“And you want my help with that, with getting her to say yes.”

“That’s right.”

Tanner seemed to be thinking it over. In any case, he sat unmoving and silent for an extended period of time. At last, he said, “I don’t want to butt in. I mean, you seem like an okay guy. But Hayley…she comes on all sweetness, with that big, bright smile. Underneath, though, she’s pure steel. She had to be strong to keep going, the way she grew up. It’s not a good idea to mess with her, you know what I’m saying?”

“I’m not asking you to mess with her.”

For the first time, Tanner smiled. He looked more like Hayley when he smiled. "Whew. Had me scared for a minute there." And he was suddenly all seriousness again. "She trusts me, okay? But she doesn't open up to me like Kelly does. I got time and grade with Kelly." Tanner's level stare assessed him. "Hayley tell you anything about our mother?"

"That she was sick a lot and had trouble keeping a job. She put Hayley in foster care. And never told her she had a brother and a sister."

"Yeah." Tanner picked up his glass then, and drank until it was empty. "She did the same to me. But I had this vague memory of a baby sister." He set down the glass. "Kelly and I are four years apart and we went into the system at the same time, right after Kelly was born. Hayley came along later. I had no idea she existed until she showed up when our mother was dying. When I was twenty-one, I finally got our mother to tell me about Kelly, who was seventeen at the time. I got the court to rule that she could come and live with me. So Kelly and me, we're close...." His voice trailed off. Marcus wondered about Kelly's kid. Who was the little ballerina's dad? Was he in the picture?

He kept his questions to himself and stuck with the main point. "I can take good care of Hayley. And our baby. Plus, she does love me. She wants to be with me. She just refuses to believe that *I* want to be with her." He slid a business card across the table. "You're a P.I. Ask around about me."

Tanner took the card. "I'll do that."

"And maybe, if you're satisfied with what you learn, you'll put in a good word for me where it counts."

"No promises."

"Fine. Whatever you can do."

"How long will you be in town?"

"As long as it takes."

"Did Hayley mention the reunion in Vegas this weekend?"

Marcus frowned. "Reunion?"

Tanner grinned. "I'll take that as a no."

Marcus said nothing. He knew his silence spoke for him.

Tanner explained, "A couple of our half brothers run resort casinos there. Impresario and High Sierra. It'll be one hell of a weekend. Bravos from all over. A Christmas family reunion."

The Las Vegas aspect was interesting. A good place for a nice, quick wedding. But by the weekend, he intended to be back in Seattle—with his bride.

Marcus admitted, "No. She hasn't mentioned it. Yet."

Tanner was giving him that measuring look again. Then he said, “Tell you what. Consider yourself invited.”

Federico was up to his old tricks in the kitchen, swearing in Spanish and throwing the pans around.

Sofia, the owner, put her hands over her ears and shouted toward the open doorway to Federico’s domain, “Will you turn it down in there? I can’t hear myself think!”

Federico only swore louder and banged another pot. The phone started ringing.

Hayley gave her boss a quick wave and headed for the back exit. Better to wait for Marcus outside, where he couldn’t hear the yelling. She pushed the door wide—and found him there already, standing by the car, not ten feet from the door.

Behind her, Sofia shouted again and more pans went clanging. The door was automatic. It took forever to shut. Hayley leaned back against it and pushed until the latch clicked.

Then, wearing her most cheerful smile, she headed toward the tall man with the scowl on his face. "You got here quick."

He went around and opened the door for her. She got in and buckled up as he went around to his side.

He stuck his key in the ignition. "What was all that screaming in there?"

She granted him a superior glance. "The chef is…temperamental. But harmless. And you're exaggerating about the screaming."

"Sounded like screaming to me," he muttered as he started the engine. "Where to?"

"Just take me to my place." She turned on the radio to a soft rock station, hoping that might keep him quiet for a while. She needed a break from his constant griping about her job, a complaint that was bound to segue into yet another proposal of marriage. Her ploy worked. The music filled the car and he drove with his mouth shut and his eyes turned to the road.

At her place, she thanked him for the ride, thinking maybe he'd let her go for the day.

Not a chance. He was right behind her when she got to her front door.

She faced him. "Look. I'm just going to get my car and go pick up a few things for the baby's room. Really boring stuff. You don't want to—"

"Why didn't you say so? Let's go."

Okay, it was sweet of him, really. To volunteer to drive her to the mall. And what else was he going to be doing in Sacramento that afternoon, anyway? "Maybe you have phone calls or something you have to make?"

"Handled."

It was the unrelenting pressure he put her under, to surrender and say yes, that was the problem. It was just so difficult to constantly say no when her poor heart kept screaming yes. She chewed on her lower lip.

And gave in. "All right. You can go with me."

"Well, of course, I'm going with you."

She raised a finger. "One condition."

"Damn it."

"Are you listening?"

"Is there a choice?"

She waited.

Finally, he grumbled, "Let me have it."

"For the rest of the day you will not mention marriage or my job."

He scowled. "What the hell?"

"Come on. It won't be so hard. Just let it be, for crying out loud. You might even enjoy yourself."

He made a scoffing sound. "I'm not here to enjoy myself."

"Hey. Go with the flow a little, why don't you, Marcus? You might be surprised."

"I don't want to be surprised."

"Fine. Have it your way. Don't be surprised. Don't enjoy yourself. Be as tense and controlling as you always are, just don't talk about my job or my marrying you. That's the deal. Take it or leave it."

"But I think that you should—"

She cut him off with an impatient sound. "Listen. Remember. No talk of marriage, no griping about my job. And you also won't tell me a single thing I *should* be doing. Agreed?"

"But if you would only…"

That time she stopped him with just a look. It was progress, of a sort. Wasn't it? She asked again, "Agreed?"

Judging by the determined set to that manly jaw of his, he wasn't the least bit pleased with her terms. Still, after several smoldering seconds, he gave her what she'd demanded.

"Agreed."

Hayley was the one who ended up being surprised. Because Marcus kept his word.

At the mall he was downright cheerful. And patient. He helped her choose a changing table, which the clerk promised would be delivered the next day. Hayley bought more receiving blankets and some onesies and rompers. He not only paid for all the baby things, he insisted on carrying the bags. And since she bought a few Christmas gifts, too, by the end of the afternoon, there were a whole bunch of bags.

They did have a little argument about who was going to buy the ballerina Barbie for DeDe and the sweater that was just perfect for Kelly. But in the end, he gave up on trying to pay for her Christmas presents and let her use her own money for those.

He was attentive, urging her to take frequent breaks to rest her tired feet. They would sit on the mall benches and talk about mundane things while the piped-in Christmas music filled the air.

Twice, his cell vibrated. He took it out and checked the display, but for once he didn't immediately start making calls or text messaging. He simply shrugged and put the phone away.

And never once did he mention her job or the *m* word.

It was…nice.

Nice. A strange word to think of in connection with Marcus Reid. Marcus was exciting. Focused. Sexy. Intense.

Nice, though?

Not hardly. Not in her experience—until that lovely, gray December day.

He bought her ice cream: mint chip in a waffle cone. They sat by the central fountain and she devoured the treat. "Good." She groaned in delight as she sucked the last of the sweet, minty coldness from the heart of the cone.

"You've got ice cream on your chin…." He dabbed at the sticky spot with the tip of his napkin—and she let him.

"Tired?" he asked when they rose and tossed their napkins in a trash bin.

She realized that she was totally exhausted. "Yeah. Ready to go home."

At her place, he carried all the bags up to her door and followed her inside. She led him to the baby's room. "Just put it all down in here for now. I'll sort it out later."

He set the pile of purchases on the floor. "A rainbow," he said as he rose. Though his back was to her, she knew he was smiling. She could hear it in his voice as he admired the mural on the wall opposite the door.

She'd had to get permission from the manager to do that mural, and to sign a paper that said she'd repaint the room a neutral color when she left—or sacrifice a substantial chunk of her deposit. "I painted it myself…." Along with the baseboard border of green grass and teddy bears.

He turned and saw her sagging against the door frame. "You're beat."

"Oh, a little. I get like this the past few

weeks. All of a sudden, I can hardly keep my head up. An hour's nap. I'll be fine...."

He put his arm around her and it felt so good—to lean on him.

She let him lead her to the other bedroom. She drooped to the bed and he slipped off her shoes for her. With a grateful sigh, she sank back into the pillows, turning on her side, the position she found the most comfortable now she was so big. He waited, his head tipped to the side, looking a little puzzled, as she slid a pillow between her knees.

"Increases blood flow," she explained. "And enhances kidney function. Good things. Trust me."

He pulled up the blanket she kept folded at the foot of the bed and settled it over her.

"I had a nice time," she told him when he tucked it in around her.

His hand brushed her cheek. “Me, too.” He said it as though he really meant it.

And she couldn’t help thinking, *If only….*

Oh, yeah. If only….

“Rest now,” he whispered, leaning closer. She looked in those green eyes and knew he would kiss her. In a vague, disconnected way she knew that she should tell him no.

But she didn’t speak. She *wanted* him to kiss her.

And then it was too late for refusals, anyway. Slowly, so gently, those wonderful lips of his settled over hers.

Chapter Five

It wasn't a long kiss.

But oh, it was one of the sweetest she'd ever shared with him. A tender kiss. A brushing kiss. A kiss that was…enough in itself, somehow.

It was a kiss that made no demands, yet a kiss that conjured memories of the fine times they'd had together. Of the busy, exhilarating days and lovely, sexy nights.

When he pulled away, she almost reached out

to hold him there. But she caught herself in time.

"We shouldn't have done that," she chided softly, speaking more to herself than to him.

"Shh. It was only a kiss."

Her eyes were drooping. She burrowed more deeply beneath the blanket and let them drift shut. Sleep claimed her instantly in its dark embrace.

Marcus left the bedroom quietly, shutting the door behind him.

He started down the hall, but found himself drawn to the baby's room. He stood in the open doorway and stared at the rainbow Hayley had painted on the far wall. It charmed him, that rainbow. It was...so like her, to paint a rainbow, a symbol of hope, on the wall of her baby's room.

She would be a good mother. Of that, he had zero doubt.

Would he—*could* he—be a good father? The question echoed uncomfortably inside his head. Until now, it had never occurred to him that he might someday be a dad. He'd thought that was for the best. The world didn't need more kids, not when so many children already grew up unwanted and unloved.

Finding Hayley pregnant, though…

Somehow, that changed everything for him, made him want exactly what he'd never expected to have, made him see at least the possibility of rainbows. Made him feel something resembling hope for the first time in a long while…

He felt a smile tug on the corners of his mouth. Damn. He'd better be careful. A day away from work and an afternoon of mall-crawling and suddenly the world seemed a brighter place. If he didn't watch himself, he'd be humming "White Christmas," stringing popcorn, watching *It's a Wonderful Life* and actually enjoying it.

His phone vibrated. He should check the display, see if it was anything important.

But he didn't. Instead, for a while longer, he stood there in the doorway to his unborn baby's room, staring at that rainbow, feeling strangely light at heart.

Hayley woke as swiftly as she'd fallen asleep. Her eyes popped open. She blinked at the bedside clock. An hour and a half had passed since she dropped off.

Marcus…

She freed a hand from the warm cocoon of the blanket and pressed her fingers to her lips. He'd kissed her, hadn't he? Just before she fell asleep. The sweetest, most tender kiss...

Really dumb. To have let him kiss her again.

Especially considering it only made her want to let him kiss her some more.

And what was that smell? Like...

Chinese food. Her stomach growled.

She sniffed the air. Oh, yeah. Definitely. Chinese. She kicked away the pillow between her knees and shoved the covers aside.

Out in the living room, she found Marcus watching *Hardball* and eating chow mein out of the carton.

He turned and their gazes locked. The familiar thrill skittered through her and the world was a golden place, bursting with promise. Right then, in the span of that shared glance, she reevaluated. Everything.

But all she said was, "What else you got in those cartons?"

"Come and see for yourself."

So she went and sat beside him and enjoyed a little popcorn shrimp and a couple of egg rolls. When they were done he put the left-overs in the fridge. She turned off the TV and waited for him to come back to the living room.

He sat down at her side. "Okay. I can hear your brain working. What are you thinking? What's going on?"

She took his hand. His eyes changed, went darker. He seemed surprised that she would make any kind of a move toward him—even such a simple thing as to clasp his hand. She heard herself admit, "Maybe I was wrong."

He put his other hand on top of hers, enclosing it between his palms. It felt really good. Cherishing, somehow. Protective. And it brought to mind the feel of his arms close around her. Funny that she always felt so safe in his embrace.

For once, he had the sense not to speak, to let her say what she meant to say in her own time.

She told him, "I had such a great time this afternoon. Truly. And it's good to be with you. I…oh, I really have missed you, the past months. I've been waiting, to get over you. To *not* miss you quite so much. But what's in my heart for you, well, it's very strong. And now you're here and you seem to really want to make things work with me…."

"I do." He said it firmly, like a vow.

And she couldn't help smiling as she gazed into those dear green eyes. "I'm thinking maybe, if we could have some time together, you and me, we might figure out if there's any chance we could make a go of it...."

"We *can* make a go of it, Hayley. Just let me—"

"Wait."

"What?"

"The time. Do you think you could give me that?"

He squeezed her hand. "You know I can. Marry me. Tomorrow. Come back with me to Seattle. We'll—"

"No. Please. Not Seattle, not yet."

"But you just said—"

"I wasn't clear. What I meant was, will you take some time off, stay here with me in Sacramento for a while?"

His face fell. "Hayley..." He said her name with real regret. "I'm sorry. I can't."

It was the answer she'd expected. She knew

how he felt about being away from his work. But she wasn't giving up yet. "Just think about it a little."

"There's nothing to think about."

"Sure, there is. Look. I know that you never take time off. You're a driven man and perfectly happy to be so. And I'm sure it's a bad time to take time off. Because it's always a bad time, really, isn't it?"

He didn't reply. There was no need. She'd just laid out his own arguments for him.

She went on, "Just…time. That's what I want from you. Stay here with me until after Christmas."

He let go of her hand. "Christmas is almost two weeks away. It's impossible. I can't—"

She interrupted, "Please. Before you start telling me all the reasons you can't, let's just talk it over. Let's explore the, er, possibilities."

"Which are?"

"There's a family reunion this weekend."

He grunted. "In Las Vegas."

She shook her head, but she was smiling. "How did you know that?"

He swore. But then he admitted, "I got hold of your brother. We had a talk. I asked him to put in a good word for me, with you. He told me about the reunion. Invited me, as a matter of fact."

"When was this?"

"Today, before I picked you up from the caterer's."

She grinned. "Working all the angles, huh?"

"Hell, yes."

She took his hand again in both of hers, turned it over, stroked his palm with her thumbs. "In the bedroom, when you kissed me…"

"Yeah?" The word was low and rough.

"I know I said we shouldn't have kissed, but what I *thought* was how much I'd missed your kisses. How I've longed for you. How I love you…."

"Then mar—"

"Don't." She touched his lips to stop the words. "Don't say it. Not now. Please. I don't want to talk about marriage. Yet. First, I want to have some time with you. I want us to be together without all the pressure and excitement and distraction of Kaffe Central. I want us to get to know each other in a whole new light. I want us to have time do nothing, except *be*."

He looked very worried. "Be. You want us to *be*."

"Tall order, huh?"

"You know how I am. I don't do *being*. I work. Hard. That's who I am."

"You let things just *be* this afternoon, didn't you? I think you did pretty well."

He reached out. She didn't duck away, but allowed him to run a finger down the curve of her cheek, to tuck a few strands of sleep-mussed hair behind her ear. To her, that touch was a pure miracle. It set off sparks along the surface of her skin, brought a tempting warmth down low in her belly.

She found she was glad. Joyous, even. That he had come to find her. That he wouldn't give up when she told him no.

His eyes had gone soft as some secret, green glen. He whispered, "Damn it, Hayley…"

Oh, yeah. Eight months pregnant and she still wanted him. Bad.

She caught his caressing hand, pressed it to her lips. And then, very gently, she let it go. "I want… honesty, with you, Marcus. And I also want us to be lovers again."

He blinked and slanted a swift glance at her huge belly. "Lovers…when?"

"Now." She laughed. "You should see your face. Too strange for you, to be the lover of a pregnant lady?"

And his eyes went all soft again. He looked almost innocent. Almost…young. "Can you?"

"Yes. If we're careful. And imaginative. If you don't mind taking it slow and easy. And if it doesn't turn you off, me being so enormous."

Again, he reached out. He touched her throat. When she shuddered and sighed, he slid his hand under her hair and caressed the back of her neck. "It doesn't turn me off. Not in the least. And I can be careful." The words were a rough caress. "And slow. And imaginative…"

"Oh, well. I really like all that in a man…"

He was looking at her mouth. "I want to kiss you."

"I want to kiss you, too...."

He picked up on her hesitation. "Okay. What's the catch?"

"Not a catch, really. But I do want honesty, between us. I think we have to start with that."

He took his hand away. "Are you saying I've lied to you?"

"Well, last night, you did say you loved me...."

He craned back from her and his eyes were watchful again—and wary.

She said, "You don't love me, do you?"

"Of course, I love—"

"Just the truth." She cut him off before he could lie again. "Please. We have to start from there."

An awful pause and then, at last, "No. I'm not in love with you. Whatever the hell that means. I'm not real crazy about the whole love thing, anyway. Love's brought me nothing but misery—and now you're mad at me, right?"

"No. Oh, no." She gulped to clear her clutching throat. "Okay. It hurts to hear you say it. But really, it's better. For you to tell me the truth."

His expression was doubtful. "If you say so."

"I just want to go into this with my eyes open, that's all. I know you're still in love with—"

"No." The word was sure and deep and final. "I'm not in love with anyone."

She didn't believe him. He *was* still in love with Adriana, even if he wouldn't let himself admit it. But she figured she'd pushed him far enough for one night. And in the end, he was an honorable man. No matter the secret yearnings in his heart, if they did get married, she knew she could trust him never to cheat on her.

And he certainly cared for her. He cared a great deal, as much as his wounded heart could bear. That much she didn't doubt. Surely, good marriages had been built on less.

"Can we move on?" he asked gruffly.

She nodded. "Let's. Where were we?"

"I was going to kiss you." He leaned in a little closer again. "Can we get back to that?"

"Oh. Kissing...."

"Objections?"

"Not a one."

"Excellent." He framed her face with gentle hands. She tipped up her lips to him, welcoming him. He smelled so good, all clean and manly, with a hint of that expensive aftershave he always wore. His mouth descended.

She felt his lips, again, on hers. At last. Nothing...nothing was as lovely as that. He brushed his mouth back and forth, teasing, tempting. And when she sighed, he took it as an invitation.

His tongue touched her lower lip. She gave a little moan and he was inside, stroking the edges of her teeth, sucking a little, making her sigh some more.

Too soon, he lifted his head. "You taste good," he said. "Better, even than I remembered…" He wrapped his hand around the nape of her neck again and he rubbed a little, massaging the bumps at the top of her spine. It felt just right, kind of eased out the tension—what was left of it, anyway, which wasn't a lot after that bone-melting kiss.

She guided his other hand to her belly. He whispered her name as he touched the high curve, his fingers spreading wide. "It feels so hard…."

"Like a watermelon, huh?"

"Is it all right if I…?"

She held his eyes. "Mmm-hmm."

He explored the shape of her, his palm curving out over the front of her, sliding inward again toward her lap.

The baby gave a nudge. "Oh!" She laughed and caught his wrist, guiding it to the side. "Wait..." She watched his face. "There. Feel that?"

His eyes held wonder. "A kick. I swear, he kicked me..."

She slanted him a teasing glance. "Could be a she, you know..."

"You didn't...find out?"

"Nope. A boy or a girl, I don't care either way. And sometimes, in life, a little mystery is good. I know he or she is healthy. So I can wait."

He kept his hand where she'd put it, waiting. "If she's a girl, she'll be pretty as her mother."

"Flattery. I like it. Tell me more."

"A little girl with red hair…"

"And green eyes," she added.

"There." His stern face seemed suddenly lit from within. "Another kick. She's athletic, no doubt about it."

She caught his hand, twined her fingers with his. "So. What do you say?"

"About what?"

"Marcus. Come *on*." Now she'd gone and proposed the impossible, she found she was eager to know if he would go for it. "Time. Over Christmas. You and me."

"Time?"

She groaned. "Stop teasing me."

He actually laughed, a rough sound. But so good to hear. And he said, "I'd have to fly back to Seattle first, get things in order there as much as possible…"

She felt warm all over, sparkly and bright. "I

can't believe this. Are you telling me I can have a whole two weeks of you away from Kaffe Central?"

"Together."

"Of course. You make it sound like a warning."

"I'm just getting things good and clear about this. I would stay here, with you."

"That's what I was hoping for."

"Could have fooled me. Until tonight."

"I think it was that kiss in the bedroom that did it."

"Damn. One little kiss. How simple is that? I should have tried it sooner."

She realized she hadn't made herself totally clear. "It would still be…I mean, it still might not work out between us. We both have to keep that in mind."

"Sorry. No."

"But you have to—"

"Uh-uh. No way. I want to marry you. *That's* what I'll be keeping in mind."

"But for the two weeks, you'll let it alone."

He grunted. "I'm not supposed to ask you to marry me again, you mean?"

She nodded. "Yes. Please. You know how you are when you get focused on something. It's a little overwhelming. I don't want to be arguing about marriage all the time."

"Right. We're supposed to just *be*."

"That's it. Consider it a hiatus. A Christmas vacation."

"For two damn weeks."

"Well?"

"Kiss me again. Then we'll see."

Chapter Six

Marcus stole more kisses before he finally gave in and agreed to try her plan.

Taking two weeks away from Seattle…

He had to be stone cold out of his mind.

But there *was* Hayley. He would have Hayley. Round, ripe, soft, sweet-smelling Hayley. She would be fully available to him, not pushing him away, no longer denying him.

She was like a drug. A good drug. The kind that made dreary days bright.

Two years ago, after Adriana left him, he'd damn well never expected to get involved with another woman—not for a long while, anyway. After all, he'd loved Adriana from some distant time in childhood. He'd always known she was the one for him, the *only* one. His perfect match. She could be cruel and self-serving. But she understood him, she *knew* him in some deep and complete way that no one else ever had.

Or so he'd always believed.

Their marriage was supposed to have lasted them a lifetime. But Adriana was restless at heart. She resented the long hours he spent at work. She called him stuffy and distant. She wanted more from him—at the same time as she said he stifled her.

In the end, the union didn't hold. She ran off to a tiny middle-European principality with a guy named VonKruger. And she filed for divorce.

He had nothing then, but the company he'd built. His job kept him going.

Until Hayley.

She tempted him. She lured him. She offered him everything—her laughter, her sweetness, her pretty, sexy body. She was a sudden warm, healing light in a life that had spiraled down to a flat baseline of hard work and gray loneliness. Because of her, what might have been a slow slide into someplace really ugly became something else altogether. With Hayley, he was as close to happy as he'd ever been.

But then it ended. He couldn't give her the love that she wanted, so she left him.

Yet now, here he was. Sitting in her living

room, agreeing to spend two weeks just *being*, whatever the hell that would entail. Funny, how a woman—the *right* woman—could make deserting the business he'd built from the ground up, the business that required his hand at the helm, seem like a perfectly reasonable idea.

But no. He knew what she'd say to that. *Not desertion, Marcus. A hiatus. A much-needed Christmas vacation….*

He kissed her some more. And he touched her. All over. It pleased him, aroused him, to feel the changes in her body. To explore the differences his baby had made.

As in the past, she held nothing back. Smiling, eyes shining, she let him undress her, let him reveal her new roundness. With no embarrassment, with only eagerness and soft sighs, she gave herself.

He was careful. It was no hardship, to be

gentle, even cautious. She needed his care now and he was only too willing to give her what she needed.

Before, sex with her had been hot and satisfying—and fun, too. Hayley was always fun. And adventurous, as well. Him on top, her on top, whatever. She'd try any position; and she enjoyed variety. Whatever he suggested, she was up for it.

And she was always ready for a little fantasy, including dress up. She'd played his French maid. And a leather-clad temptress in dangerously high heels….

He grinned to himself, remembering the fine, sexy times they'd had.

And she demanded, "Okay, what's that grin about?"

They were in her bedroom by then. Naked, together. On her bed. He cradled her breast.

Fuller than he remembered, the pale skin soft and pliant, traced now with delicate blue veins, the nipple darker than before. He lowered his head, touched his tongue to the dark red tip.

She didn't allow more, but put her hand under his chin and made him look at her again. "That grin?"

"Just…remembering. You and me. In bed. Before…"

She giggled like a little girl. "We had some fun, huh?"

He clasped her shoulder, loving the feel of her skin. Again. At last. "It was good, all right. *This* is good…"

"Oh, yeah…"

She put the pillows where she wanted them and then lay back, propped against them. He stretched out beside her and kissed her, letting his hands go roaming….

Over those swollen, tender breasts, down between them…

Again, he felt the baby move.

And then he went lower. He touched her where she was wet and waiting for him. She moaned and he deepened the kiss, as below, he stroked the soft, silky folds.

She shattered on a keening sigh. He smiled against her mouth.

"Good…" She stuck out her tongue and traced a wet trail over his lips.

He caught that tongue of hers, took it inside his mouth, and when he let go, he captured her lower lip between his teeth and bit down—gently. Until she gasped and whispered his name.

And then she found him, that soft hand of hers closing around him, tightening, holding firm, and then, oh-so-slowly sliding upward.

She caressed the tip. He moaned. She caught his mouth again and kissed him, deeply. Thoroughly. As that clever hand of hers drove him wild.

He caught her wrist just at the point where he was about to go over the edge and he trailed kisses over her cheek, giving her earlobe a tender nip before whispering what he wanted. "You. All around me. Is that safe?"

She turned her head enough to meet his lips again. "Lie down. On your back..." She breathed the words against his mouth.

And then she pushed him to his back, rising above him, that red hair falling forward over her breasts, gleaming like pure silk in the light from the lamp.

She held his eyes with hers as she took him inside her—not all the way, but enough.

Enough. Oh, yeah. More than enough.

She rode him, a slow, easy, ride, one hand tucked under her heavy stomach, for support. He held himself in check, letting her be in control. It was pure torture, holding back, not lifting his hips to her, not taking all of her, resisting the burning urge to grab her close and push in so hard and tight…

And still, though his mind whispered warnings to go gently, to take care, he couldn't resist her body's call. He felt himself rising, reaching, finding the finish in spite of the way he reined in his desire….

He let out a low, strangled sound as it took him. Fisting his hands in the sheet to keep from grabbing her, he held on, still holding back at the same time as he lost himself completely.

She moved above him, making soft sounds of encouragement, as his climax rolled through him. The world flew away. There was only her softness, her wetness, her heat.

He went where she took him, up into midnight, over the moon….

Chapter Seven

Hayley felt the bed shift as Marcus got up.

For a few lazy seconds, she kept her eyes closed, kind of drifting, still half-asleep. But eventually, she peeked.

Marcus was getting dressed.

"Hey." She sat up, shoved her hair back from her face and squinted at the clock. "It's not even six yet…."

"Gotta get a move on." He dropped to the bedside chair to put on his shoes.

She flopped back to the pillows. “Ugh. The driven business tycoon returns. I knew last night was too good to last.”

“Look who’s talking. Who’s still working when she doesn’t need to be?”

“Marcus.”

He winced. “When you say my name like that, I know there’s a lecture to follow.”

“I’m…in balance, when it comes to working. I have my job in perspective.”

“See? What’d I tell you? Next you’ll be shaking a finger at me.”

“Me? Never. Just remember. Work fast. I want you back here in time to go to the reunion with me.”

“I remember. Let the *being* begin.”

“Oh, that is exactly right.”

He frowned. “Is it safe for you to go to Las Vegas in your condition?”

She blew out a breath. “Oh, stop. Of course, it’s safe. It’s not like I’m having any problems, or even any signs of early labor.”

“Are you allowed to fly?”

“Far as I know. I think it has to be a pressurized cabin, though. Pressure changes rob the baby of oxygen, or something like that. I can check with my doctor if you’re worried.”

“Do that. If you’re good to go, we’ll take a company jet. Faster. And more comfortable. Ask your sister and brother if they want to fly with us.”

“I will. Thank you.”

He hadn’t stopped frowning. “As far as I know, they still allow smoking in Las Vegas casinos.”

“Marcus. Stop. It’s going to be fine. I’ve had no complications. This is a perfectly healthy pregnancy and the two casinos we’ll be in are new, with those amazing, state-of-the-art air filtration systems. They suck that smoke right out of the air."

"I just don't think it's good for you."

She grabbed her robe from the foot of the bed and put it on while he sat there and watched her, looking grim. "Marcus…" She waddled on over to him and held out her hand. He took it, but he still looked a long way from happy. "Stop worrying." She gave a tug. Shaking his head, he rose. She cradled his beard-rough face in her hands and went on tiptoe to kiss his scowling mouth. "Be nice and I'll make you some coffee before you go…."

"I just want you to be safe."

"I will be. I promise."

At last, he gave in and put his arms around her. They shared a sweet, slow kiss, after which she took his hand again and led him to the kitchen where the coffeepot waited.

He was gone by seven, promising to return Friday afternoon to take her to Vegas and her family reunion. She ate breakfast and got ready for work, where they had three parties that night. Amazingly, Federico was working quietly in the kitchen when she arrived. Sofia told her that she'd had a long talk with the chef. Things would be a lot less noisy around there from now on.

Hayley's trainee looked relieved.

Hayley smiled while she supervised her replacement and hummed Christmas songs under her breath. The new girl was doing fine.

And she and Marcus would have two whole weeks, together.

Who knew when she left him all those months ago, that before their baby was born, they'd be together again—for the holidays, at least?

And maybe forever. Hey. Wilder things had happened.

But she wasn't going to get ahead of herself. Uh-uh. For now, the two weeks ahead were miracle enough.

Marcus met with his managers early that afternoon. Actually, things were going damn well. The company hadn't gone under in the few days he'd been away, after all.

He explained that he was taking a two-week hiatus. *Hiatus.* He hid his smile as he said it. It sounded more…elevated, somehow, than an ordinary vacation. He told them to get together with their people. Any issue that required his input should be on his desk by six that night.

They would meet again the next morning before he left for Sacramento to handle any immediate problems. He returned to his office feeling pretty good about things. He'd have his ring on Hayley's finger before the agreed-on two weeks were up. And next month, he'd be a dad.

The dad part was damn scary. But hey. One day at a time and all that.

He spent a half hour with Joyce, clearing his calendar. Once she left him, he got down to cleaning out his in-boxes. When his BlackBerry vibrated, he figured it was probably Hayley and answered without looking at the display.

"What?" He was smiling.

"Marcus?"

Adriana. His stomach hollowed out and his pulse went racing. Damn. His hands were sweating.

He knew he should disconnect the call. He had nothing to say to her.

And yet, for reasons he didn't care to examine, he stayed on the line.

"Oh, Marcus. Are you there? Tell me you're there…."

Somehow, he found his voice. "What do you want?"

"Oh, God. How are you?"

He realized he was absolutely furious. Coldly, for the second time, he demanded, "What do you want?"

"Oh, no. I can tell from your voice. You haven't forgiven me. I'm so sorry. It was terrible, what I did. I know it. Believe me. I know it too well…."

He had a sudden gut-twisting certainty that she had returned to Seattle. "Where the hell are you?"

"London. I've left Leo."

So she'd walked out on VonKruger, too. Why wasn't he surprised?

"Oh, Marcus. I know now. I see. I've made

a horrible mistake. It was always you. Always. A nation of two, that's what we are. Nothing can change that. Our love is forever. You're alive because of me. And I can't live without you. I've been selfish and so wrong. I need to talk to you. In person. I need to *see* you."

"No."

A stunned silence, then, "You can't mean that. Tell me you'll—"

"Leave me alone, Adriana. Do not call me again."

"Oh, no. Please—"

He disconnected the call. Finally. And after that, he just sat there, holding the phone in a hand that wouldn't stop shaking, remembering....

Everything. Down all the years. In a series of knife-sharp flashing images.

You're alive because of me....

He saw himself at twelve. Skinny. Lonely. Scared. So sure that his father would kill him finally. Kill him in a drunken rage and still find some way to weasel out of facing the consequences. After all, his father was Darien Reid, heir to the Reid fortune. An important man. A man like Darien Reid didn't beat his only son to death….

It was a gray, rainy day. Like so many Seattle days. Marcus had stolen the housekeeper's stash of Darvocet and gone to school. He swallowed all the pills in the bottle, washed them down with a can of ginger ale and waited in the boys' restroom to die.

Adriana had found him.

He recalled that he came swimming up to a foggy half consciousness to find…

His head in her lap, her hair like a halo of

pure gold around her beautiful face. She had screamed at him, hadn't she? That he'd better not die, that he *couldn't* die…

The device in his hand vibrated, yanking him back from the past.

He dropped the thing to the deskpad as if it had teeth. And he waited, until it finally stopped buzzing like a furious bee and sent the caller to voice mail. Then he picked the thing up, set it on the floor and ground it into the travertine tile with the heel of his shoe.

When the phone rang at eight that night Hayley knew it would be Marcus. Her caller ID said otherwise. "Hello?"

A low chuckle, then, "Tell me you quit your job today."

"Marcus. It *is* you."

"You thought it would be some other guy?"

"No. I thought it would be you. But the number on the display is different."

"New cell number. Got a pencil?"

"The number's in my phone. Why a new one?"

"Long, boring story. Use this number from now on."

"Okay—and no, of course I didn't quit my job."

"You said you were training someone."

"Well, I am, but—"

"How are we going to be together if you're working all the time?"

Together. It sounded so good when he said it. And, well, he did have a point. "Actually, my replacement is doing really well…."

"Quit. Tomorrow."

"I wasn't planning to quit. I'm taking a six-week leave."

"And if I tell you again to quit, that will be

pushing, right? And I'm not supposed to push."

"See? You're learning."

"Start your *leave* tomorrow."

"Ever been called relentless before?"

"Frequently. Do it. Tomorrow."

All at once, she had the strangest sense that something wasn't right. Where did the feeling come from? She had no idea. He didn't sound any different, did he?

And there was nothing that he'd said....

"Hayley?"

"I'm right here."

"You all right?"

Funny he was asking *her* that question. "Fine. Truly."

"For a second there, I thought we'd lost the connection."

"Nope. And DeDe says to tell you she can't wait to ride in your jet."

"Will she be wearing her ballerina shoes?"

"Probably not. But only because Kelly won't let her."

"Your brother?"

"He'll fly with us, too. There's a big family dinner at Impresario tomorrow night to kick off the weekend. Think we can make it for that?"

"Sure. Things are in pretty good shape here. I should be there to pick you up by one tomorrow. If your sister and brother could meet us at Executive Airport around two, we can take off by two-thirty."

"I'll pass the word along."

"Did you talk to your doctor, about whether it's safe for you to be flying?"

"I talked to her nurse, will that do?"

"And her nurse said…"

"Just what I already told you. Really. I'm

fine and it's perfectly safe for me to fly in a pressurized cabin—which the jet has, right?"

"Right."

"I have to tell you. I can't wait."

"You sound like a kid at Christmas."

She laughed. "Right season. And I *feel* like a kid—well, except for the big stomach and the swollen ankles, I mean."

"You're pretty amazing." He said it so tenderly. So…admiringly. "You don't let life get you down. You don't…expect to be taken care of. I always know I can count on you. *Trust* you…"

"Thank you—and is everything all right?"

He made a low sound. "What? You get suspicious when I tell you how terrific you are?"

"No, it's just…I don't know. Nothing, I guess. As long as you're sure you're all right…"

"I am. Very much all right."

"Well. Good."

They said good-night. As soon as she hung up, she copied his new number into her address book. And then she got busy packing for the weekend trip.

Strangely, the vague feeling that something was wrong didn't go away. It lingered in the back of her mind the rest of the evening and into the night, even kept her awake for a while.

When she finally did sleep, she dreamed of the father she'd never met, of herself as a little girl, Blake Bravo looming over her, more a shadow than anything real. She whimpered in her sleep as he bent down to reach for her.

Marcus lay in bed in his house in Madison Park. He'd moved when Adriana left him, but he'd kept the same home phone number.

Big mistake.

The phone rang, as he'd known that it would. He waited through the four endless rings, until the answering machine in his office finally picked up. Once he was sure Adriana had had enough time to leave her message and hang up, he took the phone off the hook.

Before he left for California the next day, he'd make arrangements to have the number changed.

Chapter Eight

"You're a half an hour late," Hayley said when she opened the door.

Marcus shrugged. "That final meeting…"

"I know the rest. It went long. Problems?"

"Nothing my managers can't handle. I hire good people. Time I gave them a chance to show their stuff."

She reached out and took his hand and pulled him inside with her, shoving the door shut as soon as he cleared the threshold. Then she threw herself into his arms.

"Oof," he said.

She slid her hands up to encircle his neck. "A hundred and sixty pounds of pregnant person. It's a lot to hug."

"Kiss me."

So she did. A long, wet one. He lifted his mouth from hers eventually, but only to slant his head the other way.

In the end, she was the one to pull back. "If we keep on like this, we'll never get to the airport."

"You started it."

"Yeah. Wild, huh? I don't understand it. I just couldn't help myself somehow."

He looked almost misty-eyed. "It's good. This. With us."

"It is." She beamed. "Who knew, huh?"

"A second chance…" He looked…bemused.

It was so not an expression she'd ever expected to see on his face.

"Well, after all," she replied, "it's the season for miracles."

"Wow." DeDe giggled in delight. "It's like in the James Bond movies." The jet's cabin was furnished with easy chairs and tables, set up like a living area, where the Kaffe Central execs could work or relax en route. There were even bud vases mounted on the walls between the windows, each holding its own fresh-cut red rose. DeDe turned her bright eyes to her mother. "We could have martinis, shaken, not stirred."

"Only if you prove you're twenty-one first," muttered her uncle Tanner.

The grown-ups laughed and DeDe demanded to know if there would be movies.

"The screen is right there." Marcus pointed

at the spot on the ceiling from which the forty-five-inch screen would descend before the movie began.

The attendant showed DeDe to a chair, gave her a set of headphones, handed her a remote and showed her how to scan the movie choices. They all took seats and buckled up for takeoff.

Once they were in the air, DeDe had a 7-Up and chose *The Santa Clause 3* in honor of the season. She put on her headphones and settled back as the big screen came down.

Her only complaint about the trip was that it was too short. The movie wasn't over when they landed. Marcus reminded her that she could watch the rest on the way home.

High Sierra and Impresario faced each other across the Las Vegas Strip. A glass breezeway crossed the Strip five stories up, connecting the two lavish resorts. Hayley had a suite in Impresario. Kelly and DeDe were next door and Tanner two doors down along the red-and-gold carpeted hallway.

One inside their suite, Hayley and Marcus wandered together from the sitting room, with its gold-trimmed velvet sofa, to the bedroom where the enormous bed with its intricately carved headboard sat on a dais.

He said, "Kind of a French bordello effect, huh?"

"It's a Moulin Rouge theme, thank you very much."

"Oh. Well. I should have guessed."

She climbed up on the dais and perched on the bed, striking a playfully seductive pose by lacing her hands behind her head and fluttering her eyelashes. "What do you think?"

"Sexiest pregnant lady I ever saw."

She got up and went to have a look at the

bathroom. In there, it was stark and simple, very modern, the walls and floor of some gray-and-gold stone, with an open shower. The long sweep of granite counter had double sinks. The tub was big enough to swim in. And through a door by the counter, there was also a big dressing area, complete with lots of closet space, a vanity with stage-style makeup lights and a four-foot-wide floor-to-ceiling mirror.

"All courtesy of the Bravo Group," she told him as she rejoined him in the bedroom. "Ever heard of the Bravo Billionaire?" She climbed the dais again and reclaimed her spot on the bed. "Turns out he's my second cousin."

Marcus was nodding. "That's right. The famous Jonas Bravo of the L.A. Bravos. Bad Blake Bravo was his uncle…."

"Yes, he was. Four or five years ago, Jonas got together with one of my half brothers,

Aaron, who was already running High Sierra at the time. Jonas provided the funds to make High Sierra a Bravo enterprise. They brought Fletcher Bravo in when they decided to build Impresario. The way I heard it, Fletcher was running a casino in Atlantic City at the time. Had no idea at the time that he was one of us."

"Us? One of Blake Bravo's children, you mean?"

"Uh-huh."

"How many Bravos are coming for this thing?"

"Somewhere between fifty and a hundred, I think. Caitlin Bravo, one of my notorious father's many wives, put it together, with the help of her daughters-in-law. Aaron is one of Caitlin's three sons."

"Aaron. That's the one who…"

"Runs High Sierra." She laughed. "It's confusing, I know."

He mounted the dais and stood above her. "I hope someone's passing out name tags."

"Not a bad idea." She tipped her head back to look at him and a happy glow spread through her. "I'm glad. That you're here."

He sat beside her and put his arm around her. "Me, too."

She rested her head on his strong shoulder. "I started my leave from my job today."

He hugged her a little closer. "I was hoping. But you notice how I didn't ask?"

"You are becoming downright restrained."

"So glad you noticed."

Their room faced the mountains. Hayley stared out at the gray-and-purple peaks, shadowed now, as night came on, at the sprawling city that claimed the desert below. "Life has its moments, huh?"

He pressed his lips to her hair. "Yes, it does."

* * *

The dinner that night was wall-to-wall Bravos. There were speeches and toasts. And kids running everywhere. There was also a huge tree in the middle of the ballroom the family had claimed for the event. Under the tree? Presents for days.

There *were* name tags, as it turned out. A lucky thing, too.

With a new relative everywhere she turned, even Hayley had a hard time keeping them all straight—and in the months since she'd learned who her father really was, she'd made it her business to catch up on all the family relationships, to learn who Blake's wives were, who her half brothers had married and how many kids they had.

After dinner, they all pulled their chairs around the tree for a serious game of Dirty

Santa. When your name was called, you could take a gift from under the tree—or steal one that someone else had already opened and let them go to the tree again. The Bravos—kids included—showed no hesitation to snatch their relatives' presents.

Once every last package was opened, the party broke up for the evening. Some went to try their luck at the slots or the tables, some to put the kids to bed.

Tanner caught Hayley and Marcus as they were waiting for an elevator.

"We're putting together a card game in one of the private lounges over at High Sierra. Four or five tables. Texas Hold'em. You up for it, Marcus?" He sent a wry smile Hayley's way. "It's a man thing. Cigars will be smoked."

"No problem." Her back hurt, anyway, and she was beat. "I'm off to bed. Sleeping for two, you know." She brushed Marcus's shoulder. "You go ahead. Have fun."

He caught her hand, pulled her close enough to kiss the tip of her nose. "You sure you want me playing poker? Could be risky. I hear one of your brothers is a National Poker Champion."

"That would be Cade," Tanner said. "He's one of Caitlin's sons. He'll be there. But he promised to go easy on us."

Hayley grunted. "Oh, yeah. I'll just bet. Watch your wallets, boys." She went on tiptoe to give Marcus one more quick kiss. "Hand over the loot." He gave her the rhinestone-studded Las Vegas T-shirt and the set of gold-rimmed shot glasses they'd ended up with from the Dirty Santa game. "Go. Try not to lose your shirt. And don't wake me up when you come in."

"Come on." Tanner was already turning to go back the way they'd come.

Marcus hesitated. "You're sure?"

Tanner groaned. "She's positive. Let's go."

She laughed. "Did you hear me? Go!"

He fell in step with Tanner as the elevator chimed and the doors slid wide.

In the suite, Hayley stood naked by the huge, deep tub. It had steps leading down into it and a nice, big handrail to hold on to, just in case. She turned on the taps and poured in some bath gel and sat on the rim as the froth of bubbles rose higher.

At last, with a long, luxurious sigh, she sank into the silky warm water, so glad to be having a baby in the twenty-first century. In the old days, or so she'd read in the tall stack of baby books at home, people believed that sitting in bathwater during the final weeks of pregnancy could cause infection.

Not anymore. Hooray for modern medicine.

And the bathtub was truly amazing, shaped just right to relax and stretch out. There was even a fat, horseshoe-shaped pillow to cradle her neck and head. She leaned back with a sigh as one of those minor contractions—Braxton Hicks, they called them—tightened her abdomen. The cramp faded quickly. She'd been having them all day. Braxton Hicks were perfectly normal at this stage of the game. They were the mild, irregular contractions that often occurred in the final weeks before the baby was due.

Her back, though. It was really aching. She reached around and rubbed it for a while, but the pain didn't ease much. She'd pushed herself a little too hard that day and she knew it—up at six, a half day for her last day of work, the trip here, the long evening….

Tomorrow, she'd sleep late, take it nice and

easy. If she had to miss one or two of the various get-togethers Caitlin and company had planned, so be it.

She sighed and closed her eyes—and moaned when another of those fake contractions struck.

The poker game was more about the Bravo men getting together than serious card playing. There were five tables, all filled with Bravos—along with a handful of guys who'd married Bravo women: Beau from Wyoming, Mack from Florida, Logan from California and Cole Yuma, a vet from the Texas Hill Country.

Marcus started at a table with Tanner, Aaron—the one who ran High Sierra—and Brand and Brett, who were full brothers, two of the four sons of Chastity Bravo, from a tiny Northern California town called New Bethlehem Flat.

There were good cigars and excellent whisky for anyone who wanted it. Word had gotten round that Marcus and Hayley weren't married. He took a lot of friendly ribbing about how he ought to get a ring on that girl's finger and make it quick, since she looked as if she'd be having that baby any minute now.

Marcus swore he was doing the best that he could. Then he went all in on the river and won that hand. And the next hand. And the hand after that.

The hours went by. As players went out, they consolidated the tables. Marcus managed to stay in the game longer than most. But in the end, he went all in with an ace and a jack and Tucker Bravo, from Tate's Junction, Texas, beat him with a pair of sixes.

Marcus was thinking he'd call it a night

about then, head to the room and join Hayley in that big bed.

But Tanner said, “Come on, Marcus. Brett and Brand are waiting in the Forty-niner.”

“That’s a bar, right?”

“You bet.”

Since he didn’t drink, heading for a bar held little appeal. “Brett and Brand are waiting for what?”

“I told them that as soon as you had your clock cleaned at the tables, I’d drag you over there for one more round.”

“I don’t know. I’ve left your sister alone for hours now….”

Tanner grunted. “You’re pretty damn attentive. I like that in a prospective brother-in-law.”

“Thanks. I think.”

Hayley’s brother clapped him on the shoulder. “She’s sleeping. She’ll be fine.”

Since he *was* going to marry Hayley as soon as he could finish breaking down her defenses, he figured it wouldn't be a bad idea to spend a little quality time with his future in-laws. Besides, Tanner was probably right. Hayley would be sound asleep by now. It wasn't as if she'd be up there missing him.

Tanner said, "Come on, you know you're just dyin' for one last club soda."

"Two's usually my limit, but hey. I'll go for a third just this one time."

Hayley woke with a cry.

She'd dreamed of her father again—or rather, Blake Bravo's scary shadow as he loomed over her.

Her back was aching. Bad. The pain had spread, wrapping around her like strong fingers. Now it pressed hard at her abdomen, too.

She groaned as her mind surfaced through the layers of sleep—and groaned again, louder, as a hard contraction tightened her belly.

The wave of pain took over. She breathed in shallow pants as she'd learned in her labor classes. It passed at last.

And what the…?

She threw back the covers. The bed was soaking wet. She sniffed—sweet, it smelled sweet. And she was still leaking, the pale fluid sticky between her thighs.

No doubt about: her water had broken.

And she did know the signs, she'd studied up on them enough: the movement of the pain from her back around to the front; the longer, deeper, more painful contractions; the amniotic fluid streaked with pink, soaking the sheets…

She was in labor.

Chapter Nine

Marcus set down his club soda as his new PDA started vibrating. He tensed.

Adriana.

Why the hell couldn't she let it be, for God's sake?

But then again, no one had his new cell number except Hayley and Joyce, his assistant. Anyone in Seattle who needed to reach him had to go to Joyce, who would then contact him. Joyce Bowles was tough and smart. No one got by Joyce.

And that meant there was no way Adriana had charmed or cajoled his new cell number out of her.

He took out the phone and checked the display, smiling to himself when he saw it was Hayley. She must be missing him, after all.

He gave the men at the table the high sign and turned slightly away to answer. "I know it's late. I'm coming right now."

"Great. Because there's a little problem."

She sounded perfectly calm. Still, the air fled his lungs and his stomach jerked into a double knot. "Problem?"

"I think I'm having the baby."

His mind went blank as he struggled to process. The baby? She was having the baby?

Was that possible? How could that be? "Uh. Now?"

"Yes, Marcus. Now."

He said a word he shouldn't have said and he said it really loud, simultaneously bolting upright, bumping the table in the process. Two of the four drinks went over, liquor and ice splashing across the mosaic of a gold pan and pick.

The other three men shoved back their chairs and jumped up to keep from getting wet.

"Hey..."

"Watch it."

"Marcus, what the hell?"

Brand headed for the bar, presumably to get something to mop up the spilled drinks just as someone won a big jackpot somewhere in the casino. Whistles blew and bells rang.

"Marcus?" Hayley asked. He could tell by

her tone that now she was worried. For *him*. Incredible. *She* was worried about *him*. "Marcus, are you okay?"

"Hold on, sweetheart," he told her. "I'm just fine." He tipped the PDA away from his mouth and told the others, "Hayley..." He had to search for the impossible words. "She's having the baby."

She was talking again. He tried to focus on her voice. "Can you get a doctor?"

"Uh. Absolutely. No problem..."

Brand returned with a big towel and mopped up the spilled drinks as, for some unknown reason, Brett said, "Let's go have a look."

Marcus gaped at the other man. What the hell did Brett Bravo think he'd be looking at?

Brand said, "I'll get Angie. And your bag..."

"Go for it," said Brett. He spoke to Marcus.

"Let me have a word with her. We'll see where we are here."

Marcus gaped some more. The man was making zero sense.

Hayley said, "Marcus? What's going on?"

Brand was talking to him, too. "I need a room number. Are you two here, at High Sierra?"

About then, Tanner got a load of Marcus's expression. He laughed. "Easy, Marcus. Brett's a doctor. His wife Angie's a nurse."

Marcus parroted, "Doctor. Nurse. I knew that. Didn't I?"

"I heard that," Hayley said in his ear. "That's good. Tell Brett to hurry…" And then she moaned.

"Hayley. My God. Hayley…"

She panted. And groaned. "Okay. It's okay…."

It didn't sound okay to Marcus. "I'm on my way. Brett, too…" The bells rang and the whistles kept blowing. His mind was mush. He glanced wildly around, seeking the exit. And from there, which direction to the escalators and the skyway back to Impresario? Damn it to hell. He'd known the way when he got here….

Tanner gave Brand the room number. "They're at Impresario," he said.

Brand took off as the bells and whistles finally stopped.

"Let's go," said Brett.

"Hold on," Marcus told the panting, moaning woman on the other end of the line. "We're coming." Brett and Tanner fell in on either side of him. He let them lead him, handing Brett the PDA when the other man held out his hand for it.

Thank God they seemed to know the way.

In the suite, Tanner waited in the sitting room. Marcus and Brett went on into the bedroom.

They found Hayley crouched on the dais, knees drawn up, wearing one of the red terry robes provided by the hotel. Moaning.

Marcus went to her, dropped down beside her and took her hand. She kept on moaning, a hard, keening sound, and wrapped her fingers tight around his, as if clutching a lifeline.

"Oh, my darling…" he muttered and didn't know what to do next.

For some unknown reason, Brett touched the sheet, and then sniffed his hand. "What's her due date?" Marcus was busy trying to soothe Hayley and the doctor had to prompt, "Marcus? Do you know her due date?"

"Ah…January eighth."

"Less than three weeks away. She's passed the thirty-six-week mark."

"And that means?"

"The baby should be fully developed, ready to survive outside the womb. Chances are this is a normal, though slightly early, birth."

"That's good?"

"Yes. Very good. I'll be right back." And he headed for the sitting room.

What the hell? The doctor was walking away? Marcus opened his mouth to shout at him to get back over here to Hayley where he belonged. But he shut it without making a sound. He didn't want to upset Hayley any more than necessary.

"Everything's okay," he told her, though he had no idea if that was true, or not. "You heard what Brett said. A normal delivery, just a little bit early. It's all going to be fine, perfect, the baby's okay and so are you…."

He babbled on, hardly knowing what he was saying. She didn't seem to really hear him, but she clutched his hand as if letting go would be the end of her.

Seconds later, Brett returned from the sitting room. "Tanner's getting an ambulance."

"An ambulance? She needs an ambulance? I thought you said—"

"Just a precaution," Brett hurried to reassure. "Nothing to be alarmed about. If she's as far along as she seems to be, an ambulance is the best and safest way to get her to the hospital. The EMTs will be able to take care of her on the way."

"Okay," said Marcus. Total lie. At that moment, things were not okay. Not okay in a big, big way.

"Stay with her for a minute more," Brett instructed. As if he could leave her. As if he ever would. The doctor continued, "I'll scrub down as best I can. Then we'll see how far along she is."

"Yeah. Go." The doctor disappeared into the bathroom as Hayley let out a long, slow sigh.

"Marcus?" Her voice was soft, breathless.

"Right here." Her hair, sweat-soaked, clung to her clammy cheeks. He smoothed it back.

"It's...early," she said. "But not *that* early... Please don't be scared. I think it's fine." She actually smiled at him. Incredible. In her state. Smiling at him.

Before he could figure out something suitably gentle and encouraging to say to her, the doctor returned with a stack of fat, white towels from the bathroom. "Let's get rid of those wet sheets and put these down...."

Hayley seemed calmer right then, so Marcus dared to pry his fingers free of her grip. He got busy stripping the bed. When the sheets and blankets were off, they spread the towels.

"Okay," Brett said. "Hayley, let's move you up on the bed—scoot close to the edge."

Marcus helped her up and Brett examined her. He asked her how far apart her contractions were, then rattled off a string of terms that Hayley seemed to understand.

"Damn it," Marcus cut in. Since Hayley winced as if he'd startled her, he forced himself to ask in a reasonable tone, "Is she okay? Is the baby all right?"

Brett granted him a very doctorly smile. "Everything looks normal. They're both doing well."

Just as he said that, Hayley started moaning again. She slid off the bed and back onto the dais.

"Wait…no…" Marcus tried to stop her.

Brett said, "It's okay. Let her do whatever she's comfortable with. She's fine. Her body knows what it needs."

Hayley crouched on the dais, knees wide, groaning.

Brett said, “Pant. Easy. Don’t push. Remember. Easy. Not yet…”

About then, a pretty, dark-haired woman wearing jeans and a zip-up green hoodie appeared from the sitting room. She said a soft, “Hello,” as she set down a black bag and went into the bathroom.

Marcus put it together: *Angie. Brett’s wife. The nurse…*

He heard the water running in the bathroom—until Hayley’s loud groan blocked out the sound.

The nurse reappeared. Her husband stepped back as she approached Hayley on the other side.

“Angie…” Hayley managed somehow to get the word out between groans. “Thanks… for coming…”

"Glad to help."

Hayley reached for her hand and Angie gave it. Now Hayley had Marcus's fingers clasped with one hand and the nurse's with the other. Angie urged her to breathe in shallow pants—and not to push yet....

The doctor disappeared into the sitting room again.

Marcus watched him go, scowling.

Angie said, "He'll check on the ambulance."

Time slowed in the strangest way. There were moments when Hayley was calm, almost dreamy. And then she would moan again and the pain would take her.

Brett's wife stayed right with them. She said soothing things, including that Hayley was doing great.

Marcus was inordinately thankful to hear that—at the same time as he wanted to shout that this wasn't great in the least. Hayley was suffering. He hated every damn minute of her agony. He wanted to help her.

And yet he was powerless. Good only to be there, to hold her hand….

Though he'd always believed he'd never have kids, in the past week or so, Hayley had almost succeeded in convincing him that having a kid was a good thing.

Now, seeing her agony, he was sure all over again that having a kid was the worst idea nature ever dreamed up.

He didn't say that, though. It was too late to back out now. Now, he just stood by helplessly as Hayley sweated and moaned, trying to bring their baby into the world.

After forever, two guys in jumpsuits with a stretcher and more medical gear appeared. They checked Hayley over and consulted with

Brett, who'd reappeared in the bedroom when Marcus wasn't looking. At last, they helped Hayley to lie on her side on the stretcher, covered her with a blanket and started to carry her out.

Marcus followed.

One of the guys in jumpsuits said, "It'll be crowded in the van."

"Too damn bad." If all he could do was be there, he wasn't letting anyone keep him from it. "I'm going with her."

"Please," said Hayley. "Let him come…."

The paramedic stopped arguing and Brett said, "You'll need her purse—identification, insurance information…."

"Table. Sitting room," Hayley panted.

"We'll follow you," Brett promised.

Marcus grabbed her purse on the way out the door.

* * *

The paramedic had been right. They were packed in that van like sardines in a can. Marcus pressed himself against the back of the driver's seat, trying his damnedest to stay out of the way during the short, uncomfortable ride.

At the hospital, the registration process fell to Marcus. They took Hayley off to "prep" her, whatever the hell that meant. He tried to argue that he wasn't letting her go without him, but she reassured him that it would only be a few minutes and then they'd bring him back to her.

He filled out all the papers and then he waited. For endless, torturous minutes. The others—Tanner, Brett and Angie—arrived. They sat with him. Or rather, they sat and he paced.

He thought he'd lived through hell in his life. How wrong he'd been. There was no hell like the hell of waiting to be led to Hayley's side, praying she was doing all right, sure something terrible would happen while he was out here and she was in there, without him, when she needed him the most….

At last, they came and got him, gave him a hospital gown and showed him where to wash with antibacterial soap.

And then, finally, they took him to her. She reached for his hand.

The rest went by like some kind of dream—or maybe a nightmare.

Nurses and a doctor went in and out. Hayley suffered. He stayed with her, provided what comfort and encouragement he could.

Finally, the doctor said she could push.

Things happened pretty fast after that. Hayley groaned and sweated and, in agonizing increments, the miracle happened.

The doctor said, "The head has crowned. There we go. Very good. Push. Push."

The nurse said, "Here come the shoulders…."

The rest was so swift. Instantaneous, really.

He heard a baby's cry.

It was 5:17 on Saturday morning the sixteenth of December, and the doctor said, "It's a girl."

Chapter Ten

They named her Jenny, after Marcus's mother. She had a clump of dark hair on the crown of her head. Hayley said she just knew that her eyes would be green once they changed from newborn blue.

The nurses offered Marcus a rollaway bed so he could stay in the room with Hayley and the new baby. All day Saturday, they rested. Visitors were limited in order to give the new mother and her baby a chance to rest and recuperate from the birth.

Saturday afternoon, Kelly and Tanner visited briefly. They brought Marcus and Hayley their things from the suite at Impresario—along with a brand-new car seat and a diaper bag packed with all the essentials.

"The car seat's from me, so my niece will be safely buckled up when they let you out of here," Kelly said. "The diaper bag and everything in it is from Tanner."

"Don't let her kid you," muttered Tanner. "I paid for that stuff, but Kelly's the one who went out and got it all."

"However you two worked it out," Hayley said. "Thank you. You did good."

Kelly held the baby and Tanner said that everyone at the reunion sent them congratulations—and a whole bunch of baby gifts, which

Caitlin was having mailed directly to Hayley's place in Sacramento.

"When I get home, I'll send thank-you notes," Hayley said. "But for now, will you tell them how much I appreciate their thoughtfulness—how much I appreciate *them?*"

"Will do," Tanner promised.

"They're calling this little darling the Reunion Baby," Kelly said. "There have been lots of new Bravos born in the past few years. It's appropriate, I think, that there should be a new baby born at the family reunion."

After she and Tanner left, Hayley said again how glad she was to have a big family at last. "I always wanted siblings. A lot of family, that was my dream. Now I've got a big brother—and half brothers all over the country. And a sister who's also my best friend…"

Marcus couldn't resist ribbing her. "They can be dangerous, those Bravos."

"No way."

"Oh, yeah. You have to watch them at the poker table. No end to their tricks."

Hayley wasn't buying. "I know you. You held your own just fine in that card game."

"Naw. They cleaned me out."

In the hospital bassinette beside Hayley's bed, Jenny started fussing. Hayley picked her up and put her to her breast. Jenny latched right on.

Marcus watched them, the mother and the child…

His child.

He was a father now. It hardly seemed possible.

And yet, now fatherhood had happened to him, it seemed so right, somehow. As if he'd waited his whole life.

To know this one special woman.

To father this beautiful, perfect child.

When she was through nursing, Hayley passed him the baby. He cradled her with care. She hardly weighed a thing in his arms. "She's so little…."

"Not for long. Kelly says they grow up way too fast. We'll be fighting off the boyfriends before you know it."

He glanced up and their gazes met. The smile she gave him made his chest feel tight. He put on a threatening scowl. "Boyfriends? No way. Never. Not my little girl."

"I do believe all fathers with daughters say that at one time or another—at least the loving fathers do…." Her eyes held a sudden sadness. She was thinking of the father she'd never known.

"I'll be here," he vowed. "No matter what, Hayley, I'll be the best father I can be, for her.

And when you're ready, if you say yes, I'll be a true husband to you…."

She didn't say anything, only smiled a glowing, tender smile. It was enough. For now.

He turned his gaze to the baby again. "Beautiful," he said. "She is just beautiful…."

Hayley laughed. "Marcus. She's a newborn. She looks like Winston Churchill."

He spoke to the angel in his arms. "Don't you listen to her, Jenny Reid. You're gorgeous. Incredible. Completely amazing."

"Incredible and amazing. No argument there," Hayley said fondly.

Jenny puckered up her tiny mouth and then yawned. He couldn't get enough of just holding her, of looking down at her scrunched-up little face. "I wanted brothers and sisters, too," he said softly. "My mother was pregnant, when she died."

"You never told me that." Hayley's voice was so gentle. Warm. And accepting.

He looked up at her again. Her red hair, always silky, vibrant as fire, drooped in limp tendrils on her shoulders. Dark smudges of fatigue stained the skin beneath her eyes.

And yet, she was so beautiful. As beautiful as Jenny.

He said, "My father got drunk and pushed her down the stairs. It was a wide, curving staircase. And a long way down. I had snuck out of my room when I heard him yelling at her and I was crouched in the shadows at the opposite end of the landing when it happened. Neither of them knew I was there.

"My mother was…I don't know. At least six or seven months pregnant at the time. I remember she would put my hand on her big stomach and tell me how my baby brother or sister was in there."

"How unbelievably horrible for you."

"Hey. I lived. Imagine how my mother felt about it. And what about that innocent baby who never had the chance to be born? I remember my father shoving her. And she screamed when she flew backward. She hit the wall of the stairwell, bounced off. She landed on the stairs and went rolling. And rolling. All the way to the bottom where she lay so very still. I was six years old. I put my hand hard against my mouth to keep from screaming. Because I knew, if *he* knew I'd seen, he'd kill me, too.

"Later, I told my nanny. She told me that nothing of the kind had happened, that it was only a bad, bad dream I'd had because I missed my mother. I wanted to believe her. So I pretended, at least for a while, that I did believe her. That it was only a nightmare I'd had." He shut his eyes, muttered a low oath. In his mind's eye, he could still see his father's face, puffy from drinking, the whites of his eyes yellowed, traced with broken red veins. "When I got older, ten or so, I confronted him with what he'd done. He beat me. Bad. And then he said I'd better never tell a lie like that again if I wanted to keep on breathing."

"Oh, Marcus…I'm so sorry."

"My old man was monster."

"I do understand. Since mine was, too."

"I know," he said. "And I don't believe I just told you that."

"I'm glad. That you did. That you trust me that much."

He sat beside her on the edge of the bed, their daughter in his arms. "I'd do anything for you, Hayley." He glanced down at the baby. "And for Jenny…"

"Marcus." She reached out, laid her hand on

the side of his face. "I believe you would." She spoke so softly, those changeable eyes a light hazel now, brilliant as stars.

He bent near to her, the baby in his arms stirring and sighing, but not waking. "Anything..."

Hayley offered her sweet mouth and he took it. So gently. With care. He brushed his lips back and forth across hers. She sighed.

When he pulled away, she rested against the pillows and closed her eyes. He remained there beside her, holding their child, watching her face as sleep claimed her.

Guilt crept through him, stealthy. Insistent. He did have her trust now. She believed again. In him. In what they—the two of them and Jenny—could share. She believed in his honesty, that he had kept his word to her to give her only the truth.

But he hadn't been honest. Not about everything. Not about Adriana.

He should tell Hayley that Adriana had contacted him.

That she'd left the man she'd left *him* for. That she'd said she wanted to come back to him, that she thought she could reclaim what she'd tossed so carelessly away. That she believed the two of them were bound together. Forever.

He should explain that what Adriana wanted, what Adriana believed, didn't matter to him in the least.

That he was over her and the cruel kind of loving she offered, that there was no room left in his life—or his heart—for the woman who had once been his world.

He had a new world now. A better world. He wouldn't trade what he had now, with Hayley and Jenny, for anything….

Hayley stirred, sighing. And the baby in his arms, as if connected by some invisible link to her mother, stirred, as well. She made a soft, mewling sound, wrinkled up her tiny nose—and then was still, seeming to settle into a deeper sleep than before. Hayley slept on, as well.

With care, he rose and lowered the baby into her bassinet. Then he slid off his shoes and stretched out on the rollaway, shut his eyes and told his guilt and doubts to go away.

They didn't, not really. But he was just beat enough that within moments, he slept, too.

He woke when Jenny started fussing again. Hayley nursed her, though as Hayley had explained it, the first few days, the mother had no milk. The baby, she said, needed to nurse anyway, and received some special fluid that provided protection from disease and helped clean out the baby's digestive system and prepare it for real food.

It all sounded way complicated to Marcus. But if it was good for Jenny, he was all for it.

A nurse came in to perform routine examinations of Hayley and the baby. Marcus went down to the cafeteria to get some coffee. While he was out of the room, he considered turning on his PDA, seeing if he had any messages that needed dealing with immediately.

He took the device from his pocket—and then he put it back without powering it up. Today—and tomorrow—were for Hayley and Jenny. Kaffe Central could get along without him till Monday.

And if Joyce had messages from Adriana to pass on to him, he'd just as soon skip hearing about them, for now, anyway.

* * *

When the kitchen people brought up Hayley's dinner, they provided a tray for him, as well. After the meal, he and Hayley fell asleep watching TV. A couple hours later, Jenny cried and the feeding and changing process started all over again.

In the morning after breakfast, they had a visit from the doctor, who examined mother and child and said they were ready to go home that day.

"Home is Sacramento," she reminded him. "Is it all right for us to fly?"

Marcus explained that they would travel in comfort in his company's jet.

"Well, then," said the doctor. "A short flight with minimal stress. That should be perfectly safe."

Once he left them, Hayley said she was ready for a shower.

Marcus rubbed at the stubble on his jaw. "That makes two of us."

She ran a hand down her limp hair. "We're pretty scruffy, that's for sure."

"You want to go first?"

"Please."

She allowed him to carry her overnight bag in for her, but when he came back to help her, she insisted on getting there under her own steam. "Ugh." She reached the door frame and sagged against it. "I'm a wreck."

"Another day or two, you'll be good as new."

"Spoken like a man."

"Sure you don't need some help? I could scrub your back for you."

"I'll manage. Thanks." She took a step into the green-tiled room—and whipped her head around to catch him eyeing her backside, which was temptingly revealed between the ties of her hospital gown. "Don't even go there, mister."

"Hey. A man can dream."

"True. And you'll need your dreams. Because I'm never having sex again."

He laughed.

And then, slowly and stiffly, she turned around and came back toward him. When she reached him, she put her hands on his chest. "It's good to hear you laugh like that."

"Like what?"

"Like you're a happy man."

"I *am* a happy man." Damned if it wasn't true.

"I like you happy."

"You *make* me happy—and you look like you need a kiss."

"Hmm. What do you know? I believe that I do."

"But wait. I thought you just swore off sex."

"I could be convinced to rethink my position. In time...with the right kind of encouragement."

He lowered his head enough to brush his lips across hers. "Like this?"

"Umm. Perfect. More."

He wrapped his arms around her—not too tight—just enough that it could be considered an embrace. And then he kissed her again, a kiss that was still chaste, though it lasted a little longer than the one before it.

When he lifted his head, she said, "Now, see? That's what I'm talkin' about."

"The right kind of encouragement?"

"That's it. What I need. Again, please." She tipped up her mouth, offering it to him.

He kissed her again. A kiss of promise. Tender. Sweet—and just a little spicy.

When he lifted his head, she said, "Oh, yeah. Exactly what I'm looking for."

"Anything. For you."

Her smile grew wistful. "Here we are. With a baby. So much for our two weeks of just you and me…"

"Can't have everything. And Jenny's worth it."

"It's only the second day with her. It's all new and different. And we're here in our own private little world, just the three of us. With nurses and hospital staff to take care of us. Things will get challenging, believe me. Babies bring stress and change. And sleep deprivation."

"I'm willing to help. However I can."

"That could be difficult, with you in Seattle and Jenny and me in California…."

He dared to suggest, "Maybe you'll try Seattle again. Just to see how it goes."

"Maybe I will."

He took her by the shoulders. "You're serious."

"I am, yes. But even if I try moving back

to Seattle, we both know how you are. You'll get buried in work the way you always do. In the end, you'll have no time for changing diapers and rocking the baby at two in the morning."

"I'll make time, just watch me."

She looked at him sideways. "I'm not blaming you for working so hard. It's what you do best, what you love to do."

"Yeah, it is. But it's about damn time I learned how to delegate. My people are up for taking more responsibility. They've proved that in the past week."

"Marcus. You're almost convincing me that you actually want to be a hands-on kind of dad."

"That's because I do."

"You're making me think you'll try to be patient, with Jenny. With me."

Because I will."

"Then I have a question…."

"Hit me with it."

"Will you marry me?"

Chapter Eleven

At first, he was certain he hadn't heard her right. He gaped. "Uh. Huh?"

She shut her eyes and groaned. "Ohmigod. You've changed your mind, right? You've realized you don't want to marry me, after all. And you're going to say no again, just like you did in May...."

He gazed down at her scrunched-up face. She looked just like their daughter right then. "Hayley."

She kept her eyes squeezed shut and hunched up her shoulders. "Oh, God. What?"

"Look at me."

"No. I don't think so…."

He brushed a finger under her chin. "Come on. Don't be scared. Open your eyes."

"It's a bad idea. I can't take the rejection."

"Hayley…"

Finally, she opened one eye to a slit. "What?"

"Come on."

"Oh, fine. Sure. You want me looking at you while you turn me down." She opened both eyes at last. "Well?"

"Yes. Of course, I'll marry you."

She gasped. Then she frowned. "Say that again. Just the yes-word, that will do it."

"Yes."

"Oh, Marcus!" She laughed and threw her arms around his neck, wincing a little when her battered body resisted. "Now, you kiss me."

So he did. A very long kiss that time. And a deep one.

When he lifted his head, he asked, "How about here in Vegas? Today?"

She blinked. "Today? But…we're flying back to Sacramento today."

"Yeah. So?"

"It's a lot to do, all in one day. I mean, especially after having a baby yesterday."

"The jet is on call. It'll be there when we're ready for it. If we're not ready to go until nighttime, it won't be a problem. And don't worry. I'm not asking you to stand up before a justice of the peace."

"Good news. I'm seriously not up for putting on street clothes and actual shoes."

"How about this? We'll go back to Impresario. I'll get us a nice, big suite for the rest of the day. I'll arrange for a preacher or a justice of the peace—and a license. All of it. You have to know Caitlin and the others will help me get whatever we need. You can marry me in bed."

A smile broke wide across her face. "Now you're talkin'."

"With Jenny in your arms. A reunion wedding to go with the reunion baby."

"Okay. I admit it. I'm liking this."

"Hold on a minute…"

"What?"

"Don't move. Stay right there…"

"Marcus?"

He left her just long enough to go to his suitcase and take a certain small velvet box from a hidden compartment.

"You brought the ring with you, here, to Las Vegas?"

He returned to her. "What'd I say a few minutes ago? A man can dream. Give me your hand." She laid her fingers in his and he slipped the engagement ring into place.

She admired the sparkling stone. "I love it. Thank you."

"We're engaged," he said, grinning. Engaged to Hayley. The thought pleased him immensely.

She said, "It will be the world's shortest engagement, lasting…oh, maybe six hours?"

"Or less."

Hayley was still turning her hand this way and that, watching the way the enormous stone caught and reflected the light. "Did I say I love it?"

"You did—and don't worry. I've got the wedding ring, too. All ready for when you say 'I do' this afternoon."

"Talk about your whirlwind courtship."

He kissed her again. Then he took her by the shoulders and turned her toward the open bathroom door. "Now take your shower and let's get a move on."

Obediently, she trotted in there and shut the door. A moment later, he heard the water running.

He sank to the edge of the bed, hardly daring to believe that he was getting what he wanted: Hayley for a lifetime. His beautiful daughter to raise…

Adriana.

Her name came creeping, silent as a shadow, into his mind.

He should have told Hayley about the thing with Adriana. Before he said yes to her proposal.

Hayley wanted honesty. And he knew damn well she'd only proposed again because she believed she was getting just that from him: the whole truth.

He should tell her….

But then she'd worry. Maybe she'd doubt him, wonder if he really wanted to be with his ex.

The shadow of Adriana looming between them could tip the scales in the wrong direction. Hayley might decide she wanted to slow things down a little. She'd start thinking how they didn't *need* to get married today. She'd want him to explain to her why he hadn't mentioned Adriana's call earlier.

And damn it, why the hell hadn't he? It should have been a simple enough thing to say, "Adriana called me. She said she wants to try again with me. I told her no."

Simple. Direct. Clear.

But something had held him back.

And, now he really thought it over, was keeping his mouth shut about it such a bad thing?

What was the damn point in going into all that old garbage? Why couldn't they just let the past go?

He had found happiness, with Hayley and their baby. Adriana, who very well might have changed her mind again by now and returned to VonKruger, couldn't be allowed to get in the way.

Hayley could hardly believe how quickly it all was arranged.

They were married at three that afternoon.

In bed, as Marcus had promised. At Impresario, in the same suite they'd had before. Hayley wore white satin pajamas that Celia, Aaron's wife, had found for her in one of High Sierra's most exclusive boutiques. Jenny, in Hayley's arms, was wrapped in a satin-edged pink blanket with a pink, ribbon-threaded hat on her head.

Jilly, the wife of Will Bravo, who was Aaron and Cade's third brother, had scoured the bridal shops until she found a Renaissance-style circlet of greenery with white roses at the front for Hayley to wear in place of a veil. Her red hair, clean and shining now, fell loose on her shoulders. Jilly had done her makeup, too. All Hayley had to do was sit there, while Will's wife worked her magic with blusher and concealer, eyeliner and mascara.

For a woman who'd been in labor not thirty-six hours before, Hayley thought she'd cleaned up pretty damn good.

Marcus wore a tux. He wasn't actually *in* the bed, like Hayley and the baby. Rather, he sat on the edge, at Hayley's side, holding her hand. The minister stood at the foot of the bed, below the dais.

And the rest of the large, luxurious red-and-gold bedroom? It was wall-to-wall Bravos. They all came, even the kids and the babies, so many that they spilled through the arch into the sitting area.

The ceremony was brief. A quick, sentimental speech from the minister. The all-important exchange of vows.

Hayley looked in Marcus's wonderful green eyes as she said, firmly and clearly, with all the love in her overflowing heart, "I do."

Marcus slipped on the ring. It snuggled right up to the gorgeous engagement diamond. He repeated after the minister. "With this ring, I thee wed."

Then the minister said he could kiss the bride. Marcus bent close. His warm lips covered hers in a kiss so sweet and tender, it broke her heart and mended it, all in the space of a few shining seconds.

The minister said, "I now pronounce you husband and wife. Ladies and gentlemen, Hayley and Marcus Reid."

And two rooms full of Bravos erupted into applause, whistles, catcalls and cheers. Several babies, startled by the sudden shouting and clapping, began wailing.

Jenny's eyes popped open in surprise. But then she only yawned hugely and went right back to sleep.

There was champagne. And a whole bunch of toasting. Since everyone seemed to be talking at once, those giving the toasts had a little trouble being heard.

But not Caitlin. In her trademark tight jeans and sequined red shirt, she stepped up on the dais at the foot of the bed and let out a whistle so loud it had the babies wailing all over again. "Do I have your attention?"

"Go for it, Ma!" shouted Cade from the back of the room.

"You bet I will. I'm so glad you could all make it. I had one hell of a time and hope the rest of you did, too." A murmur of agreement went up. Caitlin raised her champagne high. "Here's to the bride and groom. To love and marriage. To happiness and new life. And most of all, to family." She drank.

And so did the rest of them, even the kids caught on and lifted their champagne flutes full of sparkling fruit juice.

It was a great moment, Hayley thought. And she was downright teary-eyed, to have so much family, to be married to the man she loved, with all of them there to witness their vows.

Marcus leaned close. “You look happy.”

“Oh, Marcus. I am.”

After Caitlin’s toast, things wound down swiftly. People had planes to catch, or faced a long drive home. Many took a moment to personally congratulate the newlyweds. And then, within an hour of the “I do’s,” the two rooms emptied out.

Kelly and DeDe left to get their suitcases.

“Half an hour?” Marcus asked Tanner. “I’ll have a van waiting downstairs to take us to the plane.”

“We’ll be ready.” Tanner left them.

Marcus shut the wide doors to the other room and came to sit on the bed again, next to Hayley. “How are you holding up?”

“Pretty well, all things considered.”

He leaned close and kissed her forehead, right below the crown of flowers. She freed a hand from cradling their daughter and hooked her fingers around his neck, pulling him closer, lifting her mouth. He kissed her lips.

"Umm." She stroked the hair at his temple. "I'm looking forward to a lifetime of kisses."

He smiled against her mouth. "Care for a quickie before we go?"

She stuck out her tongue and licked the seam where his lips met, just to let him know that while she might not be up for a quickie, she wasn't dead, either. "Hmm. Rain check? Ask me again in about six weeks?"

He caught several strands of her hair between his fingers and rubbed them, as if the feel of them pleased him. "That long? You're killin' me here."

"Oh, I think you'll survive."

"Maybe. Barely."

"Plus, there's how good I am with my lips and my hands."

He groaned. "Don't remind me. It's cruel."

"I can't help myself. You know how I am, a postpartum sex goddess."

"Okay. Now you're scaring me." He brushed another kiss across her lips and then, reluctantly, he pulled away. "I'll change. Then I'll help you wherever you need me."

She cast a glance at the wheelchair Marcus had rented from the hospital. "I gave you a hard time when you brought that thing with us. But now I'm so glad you did. I don't think I could make it anywhere on my own steam right now."

"We could stay another day…."

"No. Really. I can manage. I'll be on wheels the whole way to the plane. And once we board, I'll go right to sleep."

He disappeared into the dressing area.

Hayley watched him go, feeling all mushy and sentimental. She was totally exhausted. But really, her world had never been so right.

Jenny stirred, fussing. Hayley readjusted her pajama top and put her to her breast. Jenny latched on. Hayley winced. It hurt. Though the pain did ease after a moment. The books she'd studied explained that her nipples would toughen up over time—though the pain would likely get worse before it got better.

Babies. First they turned you into a walking beach ball. Then they split you open being born. And then came nursing, which could be lovely and fulfilling, the books said—*after* the nipples stopped hurting like hell.

She rubbed a gentle finger along the beautiful curve of her baby's cheek. "All worth it," she whispered. "I wouldn't change a thing…."

With a long sigh, Hayley let her head droop

back against the pillows. The corona of roses Jilly had bought for her slid down her forehead until it almost covered her eyes.

Not that she cared. Her eyes were closed anyway. She felt so very peaceful….

Marcus emerged from the dressing area five minutes later to find Hayley conked out, her crown of flowers drooping over her eyes and Jenny starting to fuss.

Hayley stirred but didn't wake when he took the crying bundle from her arms. He changed Jenny and put her in her car seat, where she waved her little hands and made soft cooing noises.

He turned to look at his new wife again. Dead to the world.

If they were going, he really did have to wake her….

He took a step toward the bed—and then changed his mind and detoured through the other room. Bracing the door with the security arm, he went out into the hallway. He knocked on Kelly's door. When she answered, he told her that Hayley was too beat to travel. "I'm just going to send you three on to Sacramento as planned. Hayley and Jenny and I will go tomorrow."

DeDe, lurking behind her mother, piped up, "Oh, Mommy, can we stay? We could go to Circus Circus. Puleeeassse!"

Kelly shushed her. "DeDe *is* out of school for the holidays and I could use an extra day off, anyway. I think we'll stay on with you and Hayley."

Marcus went down the hall and checked with Tanner, who said he was fine with staying. "Just so happens a few of my half brothers are hanging around, too. We're talking about organizing another card game for tonight. You in?"

"I'd love to, but…"

Tanner clapped him on the shoulder. "No need to explain. Go back to your bride and my new niece."

When Marcus returned to the suite, Hayley was still fast asleep. By then, the crown of flowers had drooped halfway down her nose. He took it off and set it on the night table. She didn't so much as sigh.

Jenny gurgled at him from her car seat, so he picked her up, seat and all, and carried her into the sitting room, stopping to pull the double doors shut behind him. He made some calls from the phone in there and scored a crib courtesy of Cleo Bravo, who lived on-site right there at Impresario with her husband, Fletcher, and their kids. Cleo also ran the top-quality day care the twin resorts provided for employees; she had access not only to cribs but to a whole boatload of baby stuff: blankets and sleepers and little baby T-shirts. The crib arrived, packed with baby gear, within thirty minutes of his conversation with Cleo. Marcus snapped Jenny into one of the sleepers and got her settled into her borrowed bed.

Then he stretched out on the couch and channel surfed and resisted the temptation to turn on his PDA. He was still avoiding learning if Adriana had been harassing his assistant in a continued effort to contact him.

But eventually, it was just too much free time being wasted. He could check e-mail, see how things were going at Kaffe Central while he was lying here doing nothing. He turned on his BlackBerry and checked what he dreaded most first: voice mail.

"You have one new message…."

He punched Play, and got Joyce's no-nonsense voice with a late-Friday-afternoon update. She ran down what was happening in the various departments. All good there. Everything under control. A couple of the managers had requested conference calls next week.

"But nothing urgent," Joyce said. "Strictly routine. When you get back to me, we'll set them up.

"And lastly—" Her voice changed, grew tighter, almost prim "—you received two calls today from London. Your ex-wife, she said. An Adriana VonKruger? Apparently, she's having trouble reaching you. I followed your instructions and declined to give her any of your numbers, though by the second call, she became…quite insistent. She wishes you to call her immediately." Joyce read off the number. "And that's it." Suddenly, she was laying on the brisk good cheer. "Have a good weekend, Marcus, and give me a call Monday, if you will, to set up those phone conferences for next week."

A click. And a recorded voice read the time and date stamp.

"Couldn't resist, huh?" He jerked around to see Hayley, in her white satin wedding pj's, standing in the doorway to the bedroom, eyes still drooping a little from her nap. She chuckled in a lazy, half-awake way. "You should see your face. Guilt-ee." And then she grew more serious. "Something wrong?" She spiked her fingers through that silky red hair, raking it back off her forehead.

He held up the BlackBerry and played it sheepish. "I confess. I just checked messages."

She padded over on bare feet and sat down

next to him—carefully, but a little less stiffly than before. Already, she seemed to be getting her strength back. He put an arm around her and she cuddled right into his side.

"It's okay," she teased, and kissed the side of his neck. "I forgive you. Checking messages and e-mail is definitely all right…." She gasped and jerked upright. "My God. What time is it? Don't we have to get to the plane?"

He touched her shining, sleep-messed hair. "Not happening."

"Huh?"

"We all decided to go tomorrow, instead."

"We did?"

"Yeah. Your sister and niece are heading over to Circus Circus, I believe. And Tanner and some of your half brothers are playing cards tonight." He guided her hair behind her ear, not because it needed to go there, but as an excuse to touch her. He loved touching her. It made him feel…happy. Grounded. *Right*. Who knew that he, Marcus Reid, would ever have a life that was grounded and happy?

It didn't seem possible.

But somehow, it had happened.

And nothing—and no one—was going to screw it up.

"Marcus." Her smooth brows were drawn together.

"Um?"

"You look…angry. Is something going on?"

"Not a thing."

"But you look—"

"Seriously. There's nothing. Come back here." He pulled her close again. She came to him with a sigh. He stroked her hair and ran a lazy finger down the side of her arm.

"How long was I asleep?"

"Oh, couple of hours…"

"We're staying over because of me, right?"

"Yeah. So what? Give yourself a break, woman. You had a baby yesterday."

She didn't argue, just sighed softly again and said, "Jenny's in a crib. How did that happen?"

"I called Fletcher's wife. She sent it up, along with a bunch of other baby stuff."

"I adore my family."

"They're pretty terrific, all right."

"Life's just so strange sometimes, you know? I mean, there's this crazy, bad guy named Blake Bravo. He does any number of awful, unforgivable things in his life—among them, marrying lonely women all over America and getting them pregnant, only to vanish from their lives, leaving them to do the best they can to raise his children. You'd think every one of those kids would turn out messed up and hopeless. But instead, somehow, they find love and they get married. And they have babies of their own."

He kissed the crown of her head. "Some of them have babies first and *then* get married."

"Oh, well." She snuggled in closer. "That, too. And they…find each other, you know? They find out that they have brothers. And sisters. They have a huge family, after all. When for so long they thought they were the only ones." She touched his chin and he looked down into her upturned face. "I'm so glad," she said, "to have them. And to be married to you, to have our daughter…."

"Me, too." He bent and kissed her soft lips.

In her crib, Jenny stirred. She made a fussy little noise. And then another.

Hayley groaned. "Babies. Just when you're thinking how wonderful they are, they're ready to eat again."

* * *

Later, they ordered room service and watched a movie. By nine, they were in bed.

Hayley dropped right off to sleep.

Marcus lay beside her, listening to the even sound of her breathing, knowing he needed to tell her about Adriana. They were married now. He didn't need to hold off for fear she would stall out the wedding.

He should wake her up, tell her now, get it over with.

But no. Not now. She needed her sleep.

Hayley wanted the truth from him. She *deserved* the truth and nothing less. He needed to tell her.

And he would.

Very soon.

Chapter Twelve

They landed at Sacramento Executive Airport at eleven the next morning and were back in Hayley's apartment before noon.

They got Jenny settled into her new room and ate some sandwiches. Then Hayley went back to the main bedroom to unpack and Marcus called Joyce.

He told her he'd been married over the weekend. And that his new wife had given him a daughter.

"Well," said Joyce, brisk and cheerful as ever. "Congratulations. I'm sure you'll be very happy."

"Thank you," he said. Joyce did have the basic background information. Before he left for the two-week hiatus, he'd told Joyce that there was a special woman—the one he'd had her set up accounts for—that she was pregnant and he was hoping to convince her to be his wife.

They settled on Wednesday morning for the conference calls.

Joyce asked, "You'll be staying on there for the full two weeks, then?"

He realized he wanted those two weeks now—just Hayley and Jenny and him. Away from all the pressures of his work.

And away from Adriana, should she make good on her threat to return to Seattle.

"Yes," he said. "We're just married, with a new baby. A little time away seems like a good idea."

Joyce read off his messages and he took down the phone numbers—or told her what to say when she called them back.

He waited, a sinking feeling in his gut, for her to tell him that Adriana had been calling again.

But instead, she said, "I'll speak with you Wednesday, then?"

And he realized the call was over. He said goodbye, turned off the BlackBerry, and just sat there, staring at the Christmas tree, which Hayley had plugged in the minute they walked in the door.

If Adriana had called the office again, Joyce would have told him. She was an excellent assistant. She would have made a note of it and passed it along with the rest of the messages, no matter how uncomfortable it made her to speak of the odd behavior of his ex.

So great. Terrific. He wouldn't get his hopes up or anything, but it was just possible that Adriana had finally gotten the message. Or that she'd returned to VonKruger.

Whatever. This could be the end of it. She'd never call again.

Hayley came in from the bedroom. She went straight to the tree and adjusted a wooden nutcracker ornament, anchoring it more firmly on the branch. Then she came and sat beside him.

"So? How's everything at Kaffe Central?"

He faked a look of shock. "You won't believe what's happened."

"What? Is it bad? Tell me…"

He let his mouth hang open a second more,

before confessing, "They seem to be getting along just fine without me."

She rolled her eyes. "Unbelievable."

"And yet…true."

"So. Are you saying that even though we're married and everything's settled, I still get you alone here for the rest of our two weeks?"

"Would you like that?"

"Oh, yes."

"Then, okay. You got it."

She clapped her hands like a kid. "Christmas, here. Oh, I was hoping. DeDe's got a dance recital this coming Friday."

"Can't miss that."

"And Kelly's throwing a Christmas party Saturday. I was supposed to bring the cream-cheese roll-ups."

"Wouldn't be a party without them."

She grabbed him by the shoulders. “I’m so *glad*.”

“Good.”

“And now I have this burning urge to play a bunch of Burl Ives Christmas songs.”

“Please. Anything but that.” He reeled her in and kissed her.

Then she grabbed his hand. “Come on, lazy. Since we’re staying, we need to get unpacked.”

The next day? Doctor visits. Marcus took Hayley and Jenny to the gynecologist and the pediatrician. He went into the examining room both times and held the baby when Hayley was busy with the doctor.

That night, Hayley’s milk came in. Her breasts were swollen and sore and she cried when Jenny nursed.

Marcus wanted to call the damn doctor and

see if there was something that could be done about it—and Hayley laughed through her tears.

"Oh, Marcus. It's fine, really. It's exactly the way it's supposed to be."

It didn't seem fine to him. But he let it go. He felt vaguely foolish and altogether powerless. Running a corporation was nothing compared to learning how to be a husband and father.

Wednesday Hayley went to see the caterer and tell her that she wouldn't be coming back to work there, after all. Gifts started arriving from various Bravos, and Hayley got busy on thank-you letters.

That afternoon, Joyce gave him his messages after he took his conference calls. Nothing from his ex-wife. And nothing Thursday, either. Or Friday.

By then, he was glad he'd never mentioned the thing with Adriana to Hayley. It was starting to look as though there would be no need to upset her, after all.

Friday night was DeDe's dance recital. They sat in the back of the auditorium, so that Hayley could duck out if Jenny fussed. But the baby slept right through the performance in which DeDe played minor parts in three of the dance numbers. She was a mushroom and a frog and one of Santa's elves—and what she lacked in talent, she made up for in attitude. She performed each of her tiny roles with a beaming smile and a whole lot of enthusiasm.

"She's really a terrible dancer, isn't she?" Hayley said after they got home to her apartment and put Jenny in her crib. They were on the sofa. She'd kicked off her shoes and stretched out, with her head in his lap.

"I'll say this. That kid's got a whole lot of heart."

"Yes, and heart counts. More than anything, I do believe."

He ran a finger down the side of her neck. "So what's the deal with her father? He never comes around?"

"He's long gone. His name was Michael Valutik—or Vakulic? Or something. He was Kelly's first love. They met in high school. All they had was each other, the way Kelly tells it. When they broke up, she didn't know she was pregnant."

"So then, when she found out about DeDe, did she go and tell him then?"

"She tried. She called. The line was disconnected. And then she went to the trailer where he'd lived with his mom. Strangers were living there. The trailer park manager said that his mother had died and that Michael had gone, left no forwarding address. Tanner is still looking for him. No luck, though. I think they believe he must have died or something, for him to have dropped off the face of the earth like that…."

"Maybe Tanner's not looking all that hard."

She sat up. "Marcus. Of course, he's looking hard. And he's a P.I. It's what he does for a living."

"Well, and that's my point. He would have a lot of avenues to check. There should have been *something,* some lead as to where the guy went or what happened to him."

"Well. There's not." By then, she'd retreated to the other end of the couch. "If there were, Tanner would have come up with something."

"I'm just saying, DeDe's father has a damn right to know about her."

"And I'm saying, I agree with you." She stared straight ahead—in the direction of the tree, though he knew she wasn't really looking at it. A moment later, she asked, "Is this about Jenny?" Her voice had gentled. She turned to meet his eyes again. "Because even if you'd never come to find me, you *would* have known. It was a lousy way to tell you, I realize that. But you would have gotten that letter. You would have gotten the news."

He reached for her hand. She allowed that. After a moment, she even scooted close again.

He said, low, "It's not about the letter. I'm over that."

She smiled, the sun coming out from behind gray clouds. "Whew."

"It's just..."

"Tell me."

"First love, that's all. It's a bitch. When you're young and you don't know anything and love is all that you've got...you get desperate. You make all the wrong decisions. You'll do the most crazy, self-defeating things to try and keep the one you love with you."

"Is that what happened…with you and Adriana?"

Had he actually brought up this subject? It appeared so. "I guess."

She leaned her head on his shoulder. But she didn't say anything more, didn't press him to dig up all the crap and lay it on her.

And because she didn't pressure him, he realized he *wanted* to tell her. He wanted her to understand.

How it had been. The mistakes he'd made—and maybe why he'd made them. He wanted her to have the truth of the past. It seemed important, that he should give her that.

And it came to him that he trusted her enough now to know she wouldn't misread him.

Hayley wouldn't make assumptions, wouldn't insist on injecting herself into the middle of it. She wouldn't insist on making it all about her, the way Adriana would have done.

He squeezed Hayley's hand and he said, "Adriana was…the blond-haired little girl who lived in the house down the hill and around the corner when I was small, before my mother died. She was the only daughter of my mother's best friend.

"Much later, once we became lovers and were inseparable, I told her that I'd always loved her, from the first time I saw her. I think I even had myself convinced by then that it was true. But now, looking back, I remember it differently. Adriana always had to be the center of everything. She was her mother's only girl, her father's little darling. I remember once, when we were maybe five, she hit me with one of my own toy trucks. Because I told her to leave me alone. It took six stitches to patch me up. When we were little, she hated that I didn't want anything to do with her. The more I tried to get away from her, the more she insisted on following me everywhere.

"Then my mother died. My world changed. It was me and the nannies, a series of them, and my father, who was drunk most of the time. I hardly saw Adriana after that, for three or four years, at least. Except from a distance. Now and then. We went to different private schools and her parents didn't want their precious darling mixing it up with the son of the man they suspected of murder. Twice during those years, she came to our house on her own. She knocked on the door and she demanded to see me. Both times the housekeeper called her mother, who came and took her home.

"Then, in eighth grade, her parents moved her to my school, for some reason I'm still unclear about. She fell in step with me in the hallway that first day. 'Hello, Marcus,' she said. 'Here. You can carry my books for me.' I walked faster, I pretended she wasn't there. I had this sense that once I gave her what she wanted, she would *own* me somehow. I…resisted. For weeks, I ignored her, but she wouldn't allow that. Everywhere I went, it seemed like she was always there, watching. Waiting for me to acknowledge her, to carry her books, to follow *her* around the way she was following me.

"I avoided her. Until the day I tried to commit suicide with some prescription painkillers I'd stolen from my father's housekeeper."

Hayley spoke then. "Oh, Marcus…" She squeezed his hand, but she kept her head on his shoulder and she said nothing more.

He went on. "At the time, it seemed like a good choice, to take those pills, to fall asleep and never wake up again. I thought my dad was going to kill me, anyway. I figured I'd beat him to it. Hey. I was twelve. It seemed to me that dying was the only way to escape my miserable life. I took the pills at school, in the boy's restroom. Don't ask me why I decided to off myself there."

She softly suggested, "Maybe so someone would find you. *Help* you?"

"Maybe. I must have passed out. And *she* found me. Adriana. She…saved me. And after that, well, I guess I surrendered to her, somehow. I gave her my love, such as it was. She was everything to me.

"Sometimes she was kind and mostly she wasn't. She liked the power she had over me. And she got off on…resistance, I guess. Her parents tried for the next ten years to break us up. That only made her love me more. We had what I guess you would call a stormy relationship. Always fighting and making up. It was…what I knew. *All* I knew, really. I didn't imagine there could be anything better. I didn't imagine…this."

Hayley lifted her head from the cradle of his shoulder. She didn't speak, only looked at him. A look that was so tender. And accepting. And then she laid her head back down again.

He said, "Adriana told me she was never having kids. She didn't want them. When she was eighteen, she had her tubes tied. She laughed about that, said it was a good thing, because she'd make a really bad mother, anyway."

Hayley made a low sound in her throat. "So you decided you didn't want kids, either…."

"That's right. And I believed I didn't. I was

so sure about it. Even after she ran off with VonKruger and divorced me, I was firm on that score. No children. Ever."

She raised her head again to look at him. "And you were also certain you would never marry again."

"I thought I was…dead inside. That there was nothing left to live for, with Adriana gone. But then you showed up. I couldn't resist you, which seemed really wrong, not to mention impossible. Adriana was supposed to be the only one. My life was supposed to be empty without her. But there you were, as determined as she'd been, but in a whole different way."

She looked at him steadily. "Oh, Marcus…."

He lifted her hand and kissed it. "What?"

"You're a good man. A fine man. I'm proud to be your wife. Jenny's so lucky to have you for her dad. And as for Adriana, well, she's gone off with someone else. You're free of her now."

It was his chance. The exact right moment. To tell her about the phone calls, to let her know that his ex had been…back in touch. Not because he expected to hear from Adriana again.

But because it was the right thing, the honest thing, to tell his wife.

The seconds ticked by.

"Marcus?"

"Hmm?"

"You look so…sad, suddenly."

Instead of the truth she deserved, he gave her another lie. "No. I'm not. Not sad in the least…"

"You know I'm going to hate it when you leave for Seattle," Kelly said.

"I know." Hayley spread the Christmas cloth across the table. "I'll miss you, too. A lot."

"Here we just found you—and you're leaving again. And taking my niece with you, which I find seriously annoying."

It was just the two of them in Kelly's dining room. Jenny was fast asleep in the spare room. They were setting things up for the party that night. Marcus had dropped Hayley and the baby off a half an hour before, and DeDe was at the YMCA pool with some friends.

Hayley smoothed the gold-trimmed green cloth. "I didn't expect this, I have to admit. I was all set *not* to get married."

Kelly put the empty serving dishes down. "But you're happy…."

"Yeah…"

"Okay. I'm picking up mixed signals here."

"Something's bothering him. He won't say what."

Kelly took the centerpiece of boughs and

berries from the pass-through to the kitchen and placed it in the middle of the tablecloth. "Something… serious?"

"Can't tell, since he won't say what it is."

Kelly took her hand and led her into the kitchen. They sat at the table in there. "I want to give you some really helpful advice. Unfortunately, I'm totally out of my depth here. I've never had a husband. I don't even have a boyfriend. I had sex once, though…."

Hayley laughed. "Well, I kind of figured. I mean, there's DeDe."

"No. I mean I had sex with someone other than Michael."

"Shocking."

"Yeah, right. I met this guy at a Parents Without Partners discussion group. He was an anesthesiologist. I thought, hey. Michael's been gone for six years. I need to find someone else. And this guy, he's getting out, mixing it up a little, not letting his divorce get him down. And he's got a steady job. What's not to like? We went out. An actual date. His kids were with his ex that night, so we went to his place. It was just that one time."

"You…didn't like him?"

"He was fine. It just wasn't meant to be, you know?"

"And since then?"

"Can you spell *nada?* That's it. The full extent of my expertise with relationships. My high school boyfriend, who broke my heart, gave me DeDe—and disappeared never to be heard from again. And the one-night stand with the guy from the PWP discussion group."

Hayley slanted her sister a wary look. "Are you trying to tell me something in particular?"

"Only that I'm here. I want to be helpful. But

do I have any hands-on experience with the subject in question? No."

"I'm just glad. *That* you're here."

The two of them shared a look. Fond. Sisterly. It remained a wonder to Hayley, to *have* a sister—especially a truly terrific one like Kelly.

Kelly said, "Okay, I'll take a crack at it—how 'bout this? Do you love him?"

"Passionately. Totally. Tenderly."

"Are you glad you married him?"

"Every day, every hour. With every single beat of my heart."

"Is this a deal-killer for you, this…whatever's bothering him?"

"No. Not at all."

"Have you made it clear that you're ready to listen when he's ready to start talking?"

"I think so—wait. Scratch that. I *have* made it clear. I'm sure I have."

"Is he good to you—well, I mean, so far?"

"He's amazing. He's…different than before. More attentive. Kinder. He's happy. He even said so. And if you knew him before, well, *happy* is not a word I ever would have called him in my wildest dreams."

"Are you sure you're okay with moving back to Seattle?"

"Huh? What's that got to do with something bothering *him?*"

"Never hurts to examine your own motivations a little, see if the problem might actually be yours."

"You know, for someone who claims to know zip about relationships, you're doing really well here."

"Well, there *was* that Marriage and the Family class I took when I was earning my degree."

"You must have aced it."

"As a matter of fact, I did." Kelly smiled sweetly. "Now answer the question."

"Um. Yes. I'm fine with moving back to Seattle. I like it there. I'll miss you and DeDe. And Tanner. But we'll get together. It's not *that* far away."

"Do you feel that Marcus is…opening up to you, that he's telling you what's going on inside him?"

"Funny you should ask that one. I do feel he's opening up. More and more so, every day."

"Maybe it's just a matter of time, then. Maybe you just need to be patient, let him tell you what's on his mind when *he's* ready to talk about it."

"Kelly. I am not kidding. You're really good at this."

"Thanks. But the fact remains. I haven't had sex since the anesthesiologist from the PWP discussion group. Except with myself, but that doesn't really count, now does it?"

The party that night consisted mostly of Kelly's neighbors and the people she worked with. There were also several couples whose kids went to school with DeDe.

Tanner came solo. In the kitchen, where Kelly and Hayley were taking various hot hors d'oeuvres from the oven and arranging them on serving platters, he appeared looking for a beer and then hung around to sample the crostini.

Kelly nudged him with her elbow when he reached for a roast pepper and mozzarella treat she'd just put on a plate. "If you must, would you mind eating the ones on the rack?"

He shrugged. "Fine with me." He grabbed another one and popped it into his mouth.

"And I thought you said you were bringing a date," Kelly groused.

He grunted. "Look who's talkin'."

Marcus came in and wrapped his arms around Hayley. "Jenny's sound asleep." They'd put her to bed in Kelly's room, since the spare room was the coatroom tonight.

Hayley turned her head to share a kiss with him and then went back to refilling the serving platter.

Kelly said, "You two look disgustingly happy. You almost make me want to join another discussion group."

When Hayley laughed, Tanner grunted again. "Huh? That was funny?"

"Little private joke." Kelly turned and handed him the full platter. "Here. Put this on the dining room table—and don't eat them all. Leave some for the guests."

Tanner frowned. "*I'm* a guest."

She turned him by the shoulders and gave him a push. "Go. Please." She picked up the platter that Hayley had just finished filling and followed him.

Hayley turned in the circle of her husband's arms. "Hear that?" She sang along to the CD on the stereo.... "One of my favorites."

"They're *all* your favorites." He bent his head and kissed her. A nice, long, slow one.

When they came up for air, she said, "And we're not even under the mistletoe...."

The next day was Christmas Eve. They spent it at the apartment, in their pajamas, watching holiday programming on television.

They went to bed early—and then were up again at a little after eleven, when Jenny got hungry. Once the baby was fed and changed and back in her crib, Hayley led Marcus into the living room.

She plugged in the tree and she put on a slow Christmas song and they danced in their pj's and slippers.

"It's midnight," she said, when the song was over and the stereo fell silent and it was just the two of them, standing in the middle of her living room, swaying together in the quiet. "Merry Christmas."

"Merry Christmas, my darling," he whispered.

She left him, but only long enough to play that song again.

The next morning they went to Kelly's to open presents. Then Kelly made French toast for their Christmas breakfast. They had a big turkey dinner at three that afternoon.

It was a great Christmas, Hayley thought.

The best she'd ever had. Her first Christmas with her family and it was everything she'd ever dreamed it might be.

Tuesday, the twenty-sixth, she told him at breakfast that she was going to start packing. But Marcus was having a moving company handle moving all her things.

He told her she didn't have to lift a finger.

So she took him at his word. They hung around the apartment in the morning, went out and bought groceries in the afternoon. Marcus carried Jenny and walked along beside the cart as Hayley picked up what they needed to get by for the next few days. They rented movies and sat on the couch watching them, their arms around each other.

The rest of the week went more or less the same way. They joked that they were turning into a couple of couch potatoes. Before long, they'd start calling each other Spud.

Friday came and their two weeks in Sacramento were up. But Marcus suggested they could just stay until after New Year's. It was only three more days and nothing much was going on at Kaffe Central over the big holiday weekend anyway.

As it turned out, Kelly had a party to attend at a friend's house on New Year's Eve. Tanner had a date.

So Hayley and Marcus and the baby spent the big night with DeDe at her house. They watched a Disney double feature and DeDe tried to keep her eyes open till midnight.

She didn't succeed. At eleven-thirty, she was crashed out in her nest of blankets in the family room.

On New Year's Day, they took down the tree,

put away all the decorations and packed their suitcases. Hayley felt wistful. The holidays were winding down. Tomorrow they'd be heading for Seattle.

The next day, they were in the air by eight in the morning. And at five to eleven, Marcus eased his Jaguar in next to the Hummer in the garage of the house in Madison Park.

The two-story place was just as she remembered it: Ultramodern. Gorgeous. Sleek and just a little bit sterile. So clean it squeaked because of his housekeeper who came in twice a week.

For the time being, they put Jenny's soft-sided porta-crib in the sitting area of the master suite. Hayley started unpacking and Marcus went down to his office to check his phone messages.

He was back in no time, standing in the

doorway to the combination closet/dressing room. "Three messages. One from a guy selling siding, one from the Democratic National Committee and one from the March of Dimes. I should change my number more often."

She glanced over her shoulder as she put a stack of sweaters in a drawer. "You changed the house number, too?"

"Yes, I did." He offered no explanation.

And it seemed kind of silly to ask for one. But it did strike her as odd. It wasn't as if he'd moved or anything.

He said, "I hate to leave you all alone, but I think it's probably time I checked in at work."

She went to him and slid her arms around his lean waist. "Jenny and I will be just fine."

He kissed her nose and then took one of her hands from behind his back and put a card in it. "The current alarm code and the new number here. Also, there's my number at Kaffe Central in case you've forgotten it. And if you need to go anywhere, the keys to the Hummer are—"

"The secret kitchen compartment?" There was a section of cabinet in the kitchen that held a hidden door.

He nodded. "I should be back by six."

"I doubt that."

"I'll try."

"I know you will." She kissed him goodbye and finished unpacking.

It didn't take long. There wasn't a whole lot to unpack. Most of her clothes would be coming up with the movers next week.

She had the usual mountain of baby necessities for Jenny. She put the baby stuff in one of the empty drawers in the master suite's giant closet/dressing room for now, so everything would be in easy reach.

They'd left a gray day in Sacramento. Seattle was the same, but colder, the streets and sidewalks dotted with thick patches of snow from a recent storm. Hayley sat on the end of the bed, which was bigger than king-size, had a block of brushed steel for a headboard and a quilted bedspread the color of a cloud. She stared out the big window at the gray sky and the gleaming surface of Lake Washington beneath it.

Already, she missed her tiny apartment and her old, comfortable furniture. No, none of that stuff would fit in here. Except for a few pieces she just couldn't bear to part with, the rest was already slated to be picked up in Sacramento next Tuesday by Goodwill.

She lay back with a sigh and imagined the changes she was going to make to the house. Brighter colors would do the place a world of good. And soon she'd be unpacking her personal treasures, setting them around.

When she lived here before, the place had never really felt like home. This time, it would. Hayley planned to make sure of that.

"That's it, then?" asked Marcus.

Joyce rose from the chair on the other side of his desk. "You're all caught up. I'll set up the meetings for tomorrow, as we discussed."

Again, there'd been no mention that Adriana had called. "Thanks, Joyce."

She left him.

It was now more than two weeks since his ex last tried to contact him. Adriana must have finally accepted the hard fact that he never wanted to see or hear from her again.

He was glad he'd kept his mouth shut about

the issue with Hayley. He'd gambled she didn't need to know. And he'd won.

Marcus sat back in his chair, feeling good. He was meeting with the head of the Central California expansion project for updates in half an hour. And he had a couple of high-priority calls he had to make. What remained of the day after that, he'd spend checking in with his people in person, getting anything that had strayed off the rails firmly back on track.

Hell. Maybe he'd surprise Hayley and get home by six, after all.

The doorbell chimed at a little after four, just as Hayley finished changing Jenny's diaper. She snapped the baby back into her sleeper, wrapped her in a fluffy blanket and carried her downstairs with her to the entry hall.

The bell chimed again, an impatient sound, as Hayley pulled open the wide door. The woman standing on the gray flagstone steps wore skinny black pants and high platform heels and a short, bell-shaped cashmere jacket.

She ran a slim hand back through her gorgeous mane of tawny-colored hair. "Hayley." Bored. Dismissive. Her amber-colored gaze made a slow pass over Hayley's clean-scrubbed face, her too-big sweater, her baggy cords and comfortable clogs. "Hello."

Hayley cradled her baby closer. Even if she hadn't seen pictures, she would know this woman. There was something about her: an air of privilege, the scent of money, an absolute assurance that anything she wanted would automatically be hers.

It all snapped into place for Hayley in that

instant. Her instincts had been right. Something *was* bothering Marcus.

Now she knew what.

Chapter Thirteen

"And you must be Adriana," Hayley said coolly. "Marcus has told me so much about you." She found a lovely, petty satisfaction in the look of wary surprise that crept over the blonde's perfect face. "And I'm sorry, but he isn't here right now. Try him at his office." She swung the door shut.

Adriana stuck her designer shoe in it before it closed all the way. "I came here to talk to *you*."

Hayley considered the concept of letting her

in, of hearing what she had to say. But no. That would bring nothing but Trouble. Capital *T*. "Look. I'm just not comfortable inviting you in. I don't know you—I mean, beyond what Marcus has said about you. It wasn't all that good, frankly. And he said nothing about your…stopping by today. Because I'm sure he had no idea that you were coming."

Adriana tossed her shining hair again. Even in the gray light of the winter afternoon, that hair shone with glints of pure gold. "A baby," she muttered. "I knew it, but I couldn't believe it. Marcus doesn't even *want* children. But he is so very honorable, isn't he? So he's married you. He would have felt that he *had* to. So…archaic. But that's part of his charm. Oh, what a fool that man can be."

"Please take your foot out of the door."

She kept it right where it was. "I'm back in

Seattle now. And I'm not going away. He's going to have to deal with me. I'd advise you to tell him that."

Hayley resisted the powerful urge to say something really rude. Self-control mattered in a situation like this. "Your foot. Move it. Now." Her heart was suddenly thudding in a sick, swift way and Jenny, picking up on her distress, was starting to fuss.

"You won't keep him. He's mine. And he knows it, too."

Hayley rocked the baby and pressed her lips to the velvet skin at her temple. She whispered soothingly, "Shh…"

And Marcus's ex still had her foot in the door. "I just think you should know where you stand."

Hayley patted Jenny's back and stroked her head—and spoke with a calm confidence that surprised even her. "I have nothing to say to you. And I've asked you to leave, repeatedly. This is a gated community. I have no idea why the guy in the gatehouse let you in, but you're not welcome here. Do I have to call security to get you to go?"

"Oh, please. You wouldn't dare."

"See, that's the problem, isn't it? You might have hired a detective to find out all about me. But that doesn't mean you know me. You don't have a clue what I might do."

There was a stare-down.

It surprised Hayley no end when Adriana blinked first.

She pulled her foot out of the way. "Tell Marcus he's being childish. I need to see him. And I will."

Hayley didn't waste time replying. She pushed the door shut and turned the dead bolt.

Then, since her knees felt absurdly weak,

she leaned back against the sturdy hardwood and tried to breathe normally.

Jenny let out a wail.

Hayley rubbed her tiny back and rocked her gently from side to side. "It's okay, honey. Okay. All right…"

But it was not all right.

As soon as Jenny settled down, Hayley put her in her crib. Then she picked up the phone, started to dial Marcus's cell—and hung up before she hit the final digit. This wasn't an issue to be dealt with on the phone.

She stared out the window at the gray day and wondered what she ought to do next.

Kelly…

She'd never wanted her sister as much as she did at that moment. Kelly would be at work now. But maybe Hayley would luck out and get her at a quiet moment. She reached for the phone again, half dialed her sister's cell—and stopped.

Wait. Calm down, her wiser self advised.

Really, what was she so afraid of? Marcus's ex was hardly going to break into the house and attack her. The woman had done what damage she could for the day.

And that damage was plenty.

He's going to have to deal with me. Please tell him that...he's being childish. I need to see him.

So Marcus had been refusing to see her. For how long?

Hayley knew the answer instantly: from that first night she'd sensed that something was wrong. On the phone. When she was in Sacramento and he'd come back here to Seattle to set things up for their two weeks together.

God. That was before the reunion. Almost three weeks ago.

* * *

Marcus called at seven-thirty. "I'm scum. I'm late and I know it. But I'm on my way home now."

"Great."

"Hungry? How about Italian? I can—"

"There's food here. Jenny and I went shopping." Actually, it had been therapeutic. By the time she put the groceries away, she'd started to get a little perspective on the creepy visit from Adriana.

The situation wasn't good. But it didn't have to be the end of the world unless she let it.

"I believe you are my ideal woman," he teased.

"It's only lasagna and salad."

"See? You're a mind reader. Italian. Just what I wanted. Half an hour."

"We'll be here."

He found her upstairs. She'd just fed and changed Jenny and was putting her to bed.

He came up behind her and wrapped his arms around her. "Mmm. You smell good..." He nuzzled her neck and she sighed and thought about how maybe she should wait to tell him about his ex until after he'd eaten, at least.

But really. Honesty was the deal here. To put it off any longer, to sit down to the table with him, share a meal, hear him talk about his day, to give herself time to think about how much she loved him, how she wished this problem would just go away, to possibly allow herself to put it off till later still....

That would be a lie.

And the whole point was *no lies.*

She turned in his arms.

One look in her eyes and he knew that something wasn't right. He cradled her face between his palms. "What?"

She stepped clear of his touch. "Let's go downstairs."

They sat on a beige sofa in the living room. Like the master suite above, it faced the lake, though on the ground floor, the view was framed by the winter-bare shapes of nearby trees, trees that were illuminated now by strategically placed in-ground lanterns. Here and there, in the distance, boats lit up at bow and stern bobbed on the gleaming dark water. The sky was overcast, hiding the stars.

"What?" he asked again, those straight sable brows drawn together over worried eyes.

She laid it right out there. "Adriana was here today."

He winced as if she'd struck him. And then he swore, a single, raw word.

Hayley went on, "She just showed up at the front door, out of nowhere. A…surprise visit."

His frown deepened. "How the hell did she get past the gatehouse?"

"You'll have to ask her that. She knew my name. And she knew about Jenny. She said she's moved back to Seattle now. I told her you weren't at home and she claimed that she'd come to see *me*. Then she started giving me messages to pass on to you—stuff like how you would have to deal with her. That you were being 'childish,' that she needed to see you and she wanted you to call her."

He swore again. "I damn well don't believe this."

"Yeah. Well. I hear you. I have to tell you, it freaked me out. That's one scary, determined woman. I get a bad feeling she'll go a long way to make you realize that you belong with her."

"God. Hayley. I'm so sorry. She won't bother you again. I'll make sure of it." He tried to take her hand.

She didn't allow that. "She's already been in touch with you, right?"

"Hayley—"

"Please. Just answer the question. Just tell me the truth. You know that's what I wanted. Always. The main thing, between us. Honesty. Had she already contacted you before today?"

It took him a moment. But then he finally said, "Yeah. She called me on my cell while I was back here, getting things cleared up for our two weeks together. I told her it was over, that I didn't want to get back with her. I told her never to call me again. She started calling the house."

"So you had the number changed. And your cell number, too. Because of her."

"I thought, if she couldn't reach me, she'd give it up."

"Marcus."

"Could you just not…look at me like that?"

"How can you have believed that that woman would just go away?"

"I hoped, okay? Is that such a bad thing?"

"It's unrealistic. She's…obsessed with you. I don't even know her and I wouldn't have expected her to give up. Not after what you told me about her. You said yourself she…how did you put it? She…*gets off on resistance?*"

"You don't understand."

"No. Actually, I think I do."

"What the hell is that supposed to mean?"

"You're not over her."

"Damn it. That's not true."

"Maybe you *want* to be over her, maybe you even believe that you are over her. But if you were, you would have dealt with this situation openly, you would have told me what was going on."

"I told her never to call me again. I changed my phone numbers. She's made no attempt to contact me since the Friday we went to Vegas when she called the office—twice, according to Joyce. After that, until today, nothing. I thought she'd gotten the message. I figured she'd gone back to her second husband or…moved on. Hell. I don't know. I just thought she wouldn't be bothering me anymore."

Hayley scooted farther away from him.

"Damn it, Hayley. Please…"

She put up a hand. "The question I can't get past, the thing that sticks in my brain, is why didn't you tell me? You've been lying to me for almost three weeks now."

"The hell I have."

"Marcus. You have. You know you have."

He made a low, frustrated sound. "All right. Yes. By omission."

"A lie is a lie, no matter how you try to pretty it up."

"Look. I see now I should have told you. But I really thought that there was no need for you to know."

"But there *was* a need. Between two people who are building a life together, there's *always* a need. For trust. And for truth. I don't want a life built on knowing only what you think I *need* to know. I deserve better. We both do."

Anger flared in his eyes. "There is nothing going on between Adriana and me."

"I never said there was."

"Then why are you so damn mad at me?"

"I think you know why. I've said why. More than once. And not only is there the lie you've been telling me, there's the fact that you left me swinging in the wind today."

"Hayley—"

"Uh-uh. I was not prepared to open the door and find your ex-wife standing there. I was not prepared because you didn't tell me what was going on."

"I thought it was finished."

"Adriana would say differently—and she did. This afternoon."

"Damn it, Hayley…" He let the muttered words trail off. Then he rose, went to the window and stared out over the lake. She watched as he lifted a lean arm and rubbed the back of his neck. There was something so… sad in the gesture. So infinitely weary.

God. How she loved him. So much that she'd learned to bear his not belonging to her completely. She'd learned to live—and happily—without hearing the words *I love you* from his lips.

But this…this lying. This holding back the

truth from her and then trying to convince her it had been for her own good. She just couldn't live with that.

At last, he faced her again. "You act like I've been having an affair with her or something."

"No. That's not true. I know you haven't been having an affair with her. I know you would never do such a thing. The issue is that you lied to me when you knew that honesty was what I wanted above all."

"Damn it. I didn't tell you because I knew it would upset you. Apparently, I was right."

She shook her head. "Oh, no. Uh-uh. That's not going to work on me. You don't get to hold back important information so as not to *upset* me. I'm not some wilting little flower you have to protect from real life. My father was a murdering, kidnapping, double-dealing polygamist. My mother was a basket case who wouldn't take care of me—but wouldn't let me go, either. I know a whole bunch about real life. I know how to take the hardest kind of truth."

"I said I was wrong. I *know* I was wrong. I don't know what else I can tell you. Except that I swear to you, I want nothing to do with Adriana. Since she divorced me, I've *had* nothing to do with Adriana. I spoke with her on the phone *once*, almost three weeks ago. I told her to get lost and I hung up. That's the extent of my connection with her."

"Oh, Marcus. You're not only lying to me. You're lying to yourself."

"What the—?"

"You *are* still connected to her."

"No."

"Yes. You're still not sure, what, exactly you

feel about her. You're *running* from her, Marcus. You're afraid to face her."

"That's bullsh—"

"No. Please. Think. If you had no…fears about your connection with that woman, if you were completely over her, you would have told me that she'd called you. You would have been secure in the knowledge that she was no threat to you, to me or to our marriage."

"Oh, come on. You've met her now. She's bound to make trouble, we can both see that now. She *is* a threat. Who the hell knows what she'll pull next?"

Hayley rose—because she found she couldn't sit still. "You're determined not to admit your part in this."

His face looked carved in stone—except for the furious fire that burned in his eyes. "What the hell do you want me to tell you? I've said it a thousand times. I'll say it again. I know where I stand in this. I know my part in this. I'm with you. I want to be with you. That bitch is nothing to me anymore."

She longed to believe him. But she simply didn't. "When she's nothing to you, you won't have to lie to me about her."

He swore some more. "When will you listen? When will you hear me? I feel like I'm talking to a damn brick wall." He took a step toward her.

She put out a hand. "Don't. I mean it. Just don't."

He veered the other way, headed for the back of the house.

Silent moments ticked past. She didn't hear the utility room door to the garage open and close, but she knew he was gone.

Slowly she sank to the couch again. She sat there for a long time, staring out through the naked branches of the trees, at the lake, at the lights of the boats bobbing in the darkness.

Chapter Fourteen

The days went by.

Wednesday. Thursday. Friday.

Marcus went to work early and came home late. He said nothing more about Adriana. Hayley had no idea whether or not he'd contacted the woman. She didn't ask. And he didn't tell.

The silence between them was deep and wide as an ocean, impenetrable as stone. She knew she should find a way to bridge that silence, to break through it. She knew that she'd hurt him, bad. By calling him a liar, by accusing him of still having feelings for the woman who'd left him flat for another man.

She knew that he really thought he'd been protecting her by keeping the truth from her, that he honestly believed he'd behaved honorably. She knew he would never betray her. Such behavior just wasn't in him. He was loyal to the core.

But something still bound him to Adriana. And until he admitted that was so, he would never understand the bedrock reason he'd kept the truth from her, Hayley. He would keep on lying about his own motives—to her and to himself.

She felt numb at the core, but she made herself go through the motions of living her new life as Marcus's bride. She went to the paint store and chose brighter colors for most of the rooms, made arrangements for the painters to come the following week. Once Jenny's room was painted, she planned to do a mural on one wall and a border along the baseboards, as she had at the apartment. Something cheerful and childlike—what, exactly, she hadn't decided. She sketched a number of possibilities, but she hadn't made her mind up yet which idea she'd go with.

Not a rainbow, though. Not unless she and Marcus worked out this big problem they were having first. Every time she thought of rainbows, she remembered the first time Marcus saw the rainbow in Jenny's room in Sacramento—that musing, hopeful look on his usually guarded face.

No. She couldn't do a rainbow now.

Friday night, when he finally got home from work, she lay in bed beside him, yet miles and miles away. She ached to scoot over close to him, to wrap her arms around him, to whisper, *I'm sorry. Can we please just get past this? Can we please just let it be like it was before?*

Yet somehow, she couldn't. Somehow she just wouldn't make herself apologize to him when he was the one who'd done the damage here.

And it was never going to be the way it was before. It could be better. Or worse and worse. But never the same. Those happy, magical beginning days of their marriage were gone. They'd had their first fight.

And it had been a doozy.

Yes, she did know that all relationships required compromise. A marriage that lasted necessitated give and take. At some point, one of them was going to have to make the first move, reach out a hand, try and bridge the gap.

But he hadn't done it yet. He was too angry.

And she hadn't done it—she was too hurt.

Very late, she finally drifted into a restless sleep, only to wake an hour later when Jenny started fussing in her temporary crib in the sitting room.

"I'll get her," he mumbled from way over there on the far side of the giant bed.

"No. It's all right. She's hungry. I'll do it."

In the morning, when Hayley woke, Marcus was already gone. Off to work on Saturday—which was nothing new, really. He worked long hours and she'd known that when she married him. It only seemed crappy now because of the trouble they were having.

Fussy, whiny sounds came from the sitting room. Jenny was ready to eat again.

Hayley fed and changed the baby. Then she carried her downstairs and put her in the kitchen playpen. She got the water going for tea, put the bread in the toaster and cracked a couple of eggs into a pan. The phone rang.

Her stomach clenched and her heart beat faster. Maybe it would be Marcus, making the first move toward her at last. Or it might just be Adriana, mounting another surprise attack….

The display showed it was neither. Smiling, she put the phone to her ear. “Kelly. Hey!”

Her sister teased. “What is it with you? You never call, you never write….”

Because she knew if she called Kelly, she'd only cry on her shoulder. And Kelly would worry, and she didn't want that. “Sorry. It's been a zoo around here.”

“I kind of figured. I thought I'd give you a few days to get settled in before I got in touch. I knew I'd only get all teary-eyed because I miss you so dang much. And guess what?" She made a soft little sniffling sound.

"Don't say it. I feel exactly the same way." Hayley turned off the fire under the eggs and whipped a paper towel off the roll to dab at her suddenly misty eyes. "I miss you, too. Even worse than I thought I would, and that's a whole lot."

"Hold on. I have to blow my nose." There was a loud honking sound.

Hayley laughed. "Better?"

"A little—and honestly. I didn't only call to cry over how much I miss you…."

"What's up?"

"Let me say this first. Tanner told me not to bug you. I said forget that noise. You'd want to know—and don't get all freaked on me. It's nothing that awful. Well, I mean. It's not good. But—"

"Kell."

"Yeah?"

"What is it?"

"Tanner got broadsided by a one of those humongous four-wheel-drive pickups last night."

"Omigod." Hayley pulled out a chair and sank into it. "Is he—?"

"He'll be okay. In time. Broken arm, broken leg. A couple of cracked ribs. And a concussion. The guy who hit him was totally hammered. And wouldn't you know that fool walked away without a scratch?"

"Where's Tanner now?"

"Sutter General. Under duress. You know how he is. Always on the move. Well, he won't be moving a lot for the next few weeks. And he's completely freaked because if he can't move, he can't work. He hates to miss a job and he'll miss a few with this, believe me. I keep trying to remind him that he can damn well afford this. The guy who hit him is going to be paying big-time. And besides, Tanner has insurance and money in the bank. But you know, it's not the money. It's the lack of control. Our big brother could never stand to be *not* in control."

"But he's…okay? Right?"

"Well, yeah. He'll be fine. In time."

"What about right now?"

"He hurts everywhere. He can barely move. He's one big bandage with swollen slits for eyes."

"Oh, no. That's horrible."

"And did I mention, he's really, really mad?"

Hayley stood up. "You know what? I'm not letting you guys deal with this on your own. I'll be there. I'll call you back as soon as I know when my flight gets in."

"Huh? You've got a three-week-old baby. And a brand-new husband. There's no need for you to leave your new home. Hey, it's not like he's dying. He's going to be fine. I just wanted you to know."

"Well, of course you did. I'm coming."

"Hayley, don't. There's no need for you to—"

"You already said that. I'm coming. So stop telling me not to."

She called Marcus, something she hadn't done since the big blowup Tuesday night. He surprised her by answering the phone.

"Yeah?" Cautious. And completely noncommittal.

"I, um, Kelly just called. Tanner's been in an accident."

That got a reaction. "My God. Is he okay?"

"He will be. But he's in the hospital and he's

pretty messed up. I'm going to go ahead and go down there…."

A silence. A heavy one. Then, "Of course. I'll arrange for the jet."

"Oh. Really. That's not necessary."

"As far as I'm concerned, it is. You don't want to take Jenny on a commercial flight when you don't have to."

"Marcus. She'll be fine."

"No. I'll have a car sent to get you."

"But I—"

"Two hours. Is that enough time?"

"But I said—"

"If you're taking my daughter to Sacramento, by God you'll do it in my private plane."

Well. That pretty much settled it. "All right. Two hours. I'll be ready."

"Give Tanner my best. Tell him if he needs anything, to let me know."

"I will. Yes. Absolutely."

"Have a safe trip."

"Thank you."

He hung up.

She hadn't said when she was coming home—and he hadn't asked.

"What the hell are you doing here?" Tanner growled when Hayley entered his room.

"Good to see you, too—well, except you look like holy hell." He was trussed up like a mummy, hooked up to an IV—among other things. What she could see of him didn't look good. All swollen up, battered, black-and-blue.

"Where's the baby?"

"Kelly's got her, out in the waiting room. Oh, God, Tanner..." She moved up right next to him and lightly laid her hand on his gauze-covered shoulder. "I'm so sorry. I know it must really hurt."

He made a soft snorting sort of noise. "You drag Marcus down here, too?"

"No. He stayed in Seattle."

"Well, at least one of you has some sense."

"He sent his…condolences. Said if you need anything, you should let him know."

"I need to get out of this bed and get on with my life. I've got work I need to be doing."

"Sorry. Don't think he can help you with that."

Tanner swore. "You shouldn't have come. I'll be fine. You didn't *need* to come."

"There was no way anyone could stop me."

"Well." He cleared his throat and gruffly confessed, "It's good to see you…."

She bent close enough to brush her lips on the bandage that covered his head. "Good to see you, too. You really look awful."

He chuckled—and then he moaned. "No kidding. And don't make me laugh, okay? It hurts too damn much."

Marcus sat on the neatly made bed in the master suite. It was after midnight. He'd stayed at the office as long as he could.

But eventually, he'd had to come home to this empty house.

He ran his hand over the smooth fabric of the gray quilt. Sleeping alone, without Hayley. It would be bad.

But really, how much worse could it get? The past few nights had been grim enough. In bed together, with both of them wishing they weren't.

She could have called. Just to say she'd gotten to Sacramento all right.

Though he knew that she had. She'd flown

there in his plane, after all. And he'd given orders that he was to be informed when they landed. He'd even had a car waiting, to take her to Kelly's, since Kelly had the keys to the apartment.

He stared out the window at the lights on the lake, not really seeing them, thinking that Hayley's lease wasn't up till June. Kelly was supposed to make arrangements for a sublet, and Tanner was handling selling Hayley's five-year-old compact car. The movers hadn't even picked up her things yet. And her furniture was still there, wasn't it?

She could walk right back into her old life without missing a beat. If that was her plan.

Had she left him? Was that what was really going on here?

He shut his eyes, blocking out the sight of the lake, closing his mind off from the idea that she wasn't coming back, that he could have lost her, that their future consisted of a divorce and a custody agreement.

Give it time, he thought. *We both just need a little damn time.*

Hayley made herself call Marcus the next morning at eight.

"Hey," she said after his hello.

"Hey. So. You got in all right."

"Perfect. Thanks for arranging for the car."

"No problem. How's Tanner?"

"He's a mess. And he's mad. He'll be flat on his back for a while."

"But he'll be okay, in the end?"

"Yeah. He'll pull through fine. The doctors say everything should heal up good as new."

"Tell him to take it easy."

"It's not like he has a choice—but yeah. I will."

"How's Jenny?"

"Fine."

"Good."

"I'm…well, I think I'll stay on here. Stick by Tanner, until he gets through the worst of this…." Tomorrow she would call Goodwill and the movers, let them know she was putting off clearing out the apartment. And she would also call the painters up in Seattle, tell them she was canceling the job for now. She added, "It's just for a while…."

"A while," he repeated. But he didn't ask how long a while might be. The silence stretched. And then he said, "All right, then. Goodbye."

And the line went dead.

Hayley clutched the phone against her chest. She should call him again. Right now. Tell him she'd changed her mind, she was coming home tomorrow. She should say that she hated what was happening between them and she longed only to work things out, make it better, make the silence and the distance go away.

But then Jenny cried.

Hayley set down the phone and went to get her. And somehow, later, Hayley couldn't quite bring herself to make that second call.

Two weeks went by before Kelly started asking questions. Tanner was out of the hospital by then, getting around on crutches with great difficulty, since he also had that broken arm, constantly complaining but also swiftly improving.

It was Saturday. The sisters sat at the round table in Kelly's kitchen. Jenny cooed in her bouncy seat and DeDe was down the street at a girlfriend's. Candy, DeDe's ancient dog, lay curled on the rug in the corner.

Chocolate chip cookies cooled on a rack on

the counter and a plate of them, still warm, sat on the table within easy reach.

"Okay," said Kelly. "I keep trying to figure out a smooth way to say this…." Hayley knew what was coming. It was. "What's going on? Is there a problem between you and Marcus?"

Hayley stared into her mug of decaf. "Long story."

Kelly waited for her to continue. But she didn't. "What? You don't want to talk about it."

Slowly, Hayley shook her head. Then she made herself meet her sister's eyes. "Thanks. No."

"God, Hayley. I don't like this. I worry, you know?" Kelly's hand rested on the table.

Hayley put her own hand over it. "Don't. It'll all work out."

Would it? It didn't really look that way.

Everything was all wrong, yet Hayley did

nothing. She took care of her baby and spent time with her family.

She was waiting. But for what?

She had absolutely no idea.

Two weeks and two days after Hayley took Jenny and went back to Sacramento, Adriana started calling Marcus again. On his new cell number.

It wasn't a surprise. Whatever detective she'd hired would have found his new numbers for her.

He lucked out the first time she called. He was in a meeting, so she got bumped to voice mail.

Later, when he checked messages, hers was waiting.

"I know that she's left you, Marcus, that she took that baby you didn't even want and went back to California. I know everything. And I've been waiting. For your call. But I can see you've decided to continue being stubborn. To make me pay. Because of Leo. Fine. I'm a patient woman. Within reason. But eventually you will have to come to me. And when you do—"

He stopped the damn thing there and erased it. He didn't need to hear the rest. He knew it already. It was pretty much the same message she'd been sending since he was four years old.

After that, he checked the display before he picked up any ringing phones. She left a lot of messages. He never played a single one of them back, just hit Delete and got on with his life.

Such as it was.

Sunday, the twenty-eighth of January, Jenny was six weeks old. Kelly offered Sunday dinner and Hayley was happy to accept.

After the meal, Hayley used the spare room

to feed Jenny. The baby was through eating and Hayley was changing her on the bed when there was a tap on the door.

"Come on in."

It was Tanner. Leaning on his crutches, he stuck his head in. "Got a minute?"

She pressed the tabs on Jenny's diaper. "Sure."

He hobbled in, braced both crutches against the wall and shut the door behind him. His arm had healed quickly, but he still wasn't comfortable putting much weight on his broken leg. He leaned against the door frame for support. "Hayley…" He looked down at the floor, or maybe at the removable cast.

"All right." She snapped Jenny into a sleeper. "What's the matter?"

He cleared his throat and lifted his dark head with some reluctance. "Kelly and me, we're worried about you. And Marcus."

She picked up the baby and put her on her shoulder. Gently, she rubbed her little back. Jenny yawned and put her head down with a contented sigh. In a minute, she'd be sound asleep, ready for a long nap in the playpen Kelly kept in the corner for Jenny's use when they visited.

It took so little to make a baby happy: food, a clean diaper, a pair of loving arms….

"Please don't worry," Hayley said. "Yes, we're having problems, Marcus and me. But there's nothing you or Kelly can do about it."

"Kelly says you won't talk about it."

"That's right. I…well, talking won't solve anything. I've got nothing to say, really."

Tanner frowned. "I don't believe that. I mean, don't women need that, to talk? I never met a woman who didn't have a whole hell of a lot to say about whatever was bothering her."

"Tanner." She shook her head. "You get the feeling you're out of your depth here?"

He actually chuckled. "Oh, well. Yeah. Guess I am—but I just wanted you to know..."

"What?"

"Well, I could call the guy. Have a talk with him, if you think maybe that will help."

"And say...what?"

"Hell. Whatever you want me to say."

"It's good—" she gave him a smile "—to have a big brother."

He grunted. "Glad you feel that way. And you didn't answer my question. Want me to have a talk with him?"

"No. But I do appreciate that you care. That you want to help. Right now, though, there's nothing you can do."

"I can break his face in. How 'bout that?"

She chuckled. "Not an especially constructive approach."

"Damn it. I hate to see you hurting."

"Thanks. But it's my problem."

"Gotta tell ya. You don't seem like you're doing a whole lot to work it out."

"Tanner. My problem."

He muttered a swearword. "You're damn stubborn, you know that?"

"Maybe."

"Uh-uh. No maybe about it. When you finally get ready to, will you talk to Kelly?"

"I will. I promise."

He jumped on his good foot as he levered his crutches under his arms. "Well. Guess there's nothing else to say…."

"I mean it. Thank you. For trying. For… caring."

"Work this out," he commanded gruffly.

She only smiled at him fondly and turned to put Jenny in the playpen.

The next day, Hayley went to see her gynecologist for her postpartum checkup.

She got a clean bill of health and a prescription for progestin-only birth control pills, which were safe for nursing mothers. The doctor told her to begin taking the pills right away. She'd be fully protected against pregnancy within a month. And the doctor also gave Hayley a complimentary box of condoms to use until the pills took effect.

Great. She was ready for anything, free to have all-the-way, unrestricted, wild and wonderful sex at last. Too bad there was no one to have sex with—unrestricted or otherwise.

It was just so pathetic. At home, Hayley put Jenny down for a nap and then sat on her bed and cried.

The waterworks didn't help in the least. Finally, after sobbing for an hour, she called Kelly, who came over during her lunch break.

Hayley told all.

Kelly handed her yet another tissue and declared, "Sorry. I don't believe that husband of yours is, was, or ever will be cheating on you."

Hayley blew her nose for the hundredth time that day. "I know he hasn't cheated. That's not the point."

"O-kay. Then the point is…?"

"Kelly. He lied to me. It's the one thing I wanted from him, the one thing I asked for. Honesty. But still. He lied."

"That's right. He lied. He tried to protect you from his psycho ex-wife. And then, when he thought he was rid of her, he decided to just let the whole thing go rather than worry you. Is that so terrible?"

"God. You sound just like him."

"Well, I'm only saying, look at it from his point of view."

Hayley rubbed her red eyes. "There's more to it than that. He loved that woman. He gave her everything. He believed that she would always be the only one for him. I think, deep down, maybe he still believes it."

"EEEuuu. You think he wants to get back with her? Please. He couldn't be that self-destructive."

"It's…complicated. Remember I told you the guy had one of those hell-on-earth childhoods?"

"And we didn't?"

"His was worse."

"Than ours? Not possible."

"But true. And to answer your question, no. I don't think he wants to get back with her."

"Well, good. You kind of had me scared there

for a minute. I mean, no way you should think that. It's so painfully clear that the guy's crazy in love with you."

Hayley felt the tears rising all over again. "Oh, don't I wish." She grabbed another tissue and blotted her eyes.

Her sister said, "You've got to go back to him, work this out. Time goes by, you know? You stay here, he stays there. You're only going to drift farther and farther apart…."

"I know. You're right. I know…"

Yet somehow, another week went by and Hayley did nothing to reach out to her husband. By then, they'd been apart for a month.

She was mindful of Kelly's warnings. And she did long to go to him.

But stronger than her yearning was her fear of what she might find when she got there.

* * *

Even a workaholic can't work late *every* night.

For the first time since Hayley left him, Marcus got home at six. He changed into jeans and a sweater and he heated up the meal his housekeeper had left for him.

He ate. He was just putting the plate in the dishwasher when the doorbell chimed.

His heart turned over. *Hayley.*

But no. She had a key. No need to ring the bell…

His pulse settled back into its regular dull rhythm.

The bell chimed again when he reached the front of the house. He knew by then who it would be.

He realized it was time. He was ready at last. He pulled the door open.

On the other side, Adriana looked at him

meltingly. Behind her, beyond the porch, snow swirled in the icy dark.

"Oh, Marcus. At last." She wore a leather trench coat and impossibly high heels and her hair sparkled, dusted with snow. She looked like something out of some old Hollywood movie. Something…unreal.

He looked into those wide, whiskey-colored eyes and felt absolutely nothing. He might as well have been looking at a picture of a model in some fashion magazine. Objectively, he saw how stunning she was, a portrait of feminine perfection.

But what did she have to do with him? Not a thing. It seemed so strange to him, that he'd once been married to her.

The truth came clear to him, in that instant.

Adriana Carlson had never had any power over him that he hadn't given her, hadn't handed over, like an offering. Like a sacrifice.

He stepped back. She entered the foyer. He shut the door.

"Oh, at last, at last…" She reached for him.

He took a second step backward, free of her grasping touch.

"Oh!" The huge brown eyes filled with tragic tears. She pressed the back of her slim hand to her mouth. "Oh, what do I have to do? How can I show you I know I was wrong? We need to stop this. You know that we do. We need to heal this horrible breach between us, so we can be together again."

"Adriana. Cut the crap, okay?"

She gasped. It was very dramatic. "What? I don't know what you—"

"Yeah. You do. You know exactly what I mean. You've got some wild idea that I still have feelings for you. You're wrong. I don't. I love my wife." *I love my wife.*

Had he really said those words?

Oh, yeah. He had.

And they were true.

Damn. What a hopeless, witless idiot he'd been.

Hayley. He loved Hayley. For months now, he'd loved her.

Since well before she left him that first time, back in May.

How many times was he going to let her leave him? How many times did he have to lose her, before he finally got a clue and admitted that she was the one for him? That he loved her, would always love her.

That this thing with Adriana was truly over.

There was no room for that old, tortured love in his heart now. How could there be? His heart was filled.

With light. With hope. With goodness.

With Hayley.

Adriana gasped again. Strangely, that second time, her gasp almost sounded real. "You're serious…." It came out in a stunned whisper.

He reached for the door again and pulled it open. "Please don't bother me, or Hayley, anymore. There's no point. She has my heart. I belong to her. Do you see that now?"

"I…" She put her hand to her mouth again, and then let it fall. And then, at last, she said it. She admitted it. "Yes. All right. I see." She turned and stepped out into the snowy darkness.

He shut the door behind her.

There were bells ringing.

Hayley groaned and rolled over.

The bells rang some more.

She opened one eye. It was pitch-dark in her

bedroom, except for the glow of the digital clock, which said it was five minutes of midnight.

Five minutes of midnight.

And some fool was ringing her doorbell.

The fool rang it again. Any second now, Jenny would start crying.

Hayley turned on the light, threw back the covers, shoved her feet into her waiting slippers, grabbed her old robe from the end of the bed and raced to the front door. She couldn't wait to yank it wide and give the idiot on the other side a large piece of her mind.

Hayley glared through the peephole before turning the lock. What she saw made her throat clutch and her knees tremble.

Marcus.

Chapter Fifteen

Hayley's hand shook as she turned the dead bolt. She flung the door wide.

He was wearing old jeans, a tan sweater and a heavy leather jacket. He looked…amazing.

She wanted to throw herself at him, wrap her arms tight around him, kiss him and kiss him. Hold him forever. Tell him how very much she'd missed him, promise him her love and her undying devotion. Swear to him that now he'd come to get her at last, she would never, ever let him go.

But *had* he come to work things out?

Or to tell her it was over?

Oh, Lord. Why didn't he say something?

Why didn't *she* say something?

A terrible shyness had overtaken her. So many of those passionate things she yearned to tell him. But somehow, her throat had locked up tight and her lips had got to trembling—*all* of her was trembling. She could only wrap her arms around herself, only swallow and shiver and stare.

They stood there in the near-freezing middle of the night, in the open doorway, just looking at each other.

He was the one who finally spoke. "I know it's late. I guess I should have called and warned you I was coming, but…" The sentence wandered off. He showed no inclination to finish it. "You're shaking…" He reached for her.

She lifted on tiptoe and swayed longingly toward him.

But the contact didn't quite happen. His hand dropped to his side at the same time as she caught herself and drew back, settling onto her heels again with a sad little sigh.

They stared at each other. She felt absolutely miserable. Judging by his bleak expression, he did, too.

He asked, "Are you all right?"

Somehow, she managed to croak, "Yes… No… Oh, God. I don't know…."

"Is it okay if I come in?"

She swallowed again, and bobbed her head. "Yes. How silly. Of course you should come in." Somehow she made her shaking legs move, stepping back enough to clear the doorway.

He entered.

She shut the door, turned the lock. “Your jacket…”

He handed it over. She hung it in the closet.

And another unbearable silence ensued, a silence thick with all the things neither of them seemed to know how to say.

She had the strangest sense that they were making a kind of progress toward something monumental, and they were doing this in tiny steps, by slow, agonized degrees.

“Uh, how’s Tanner?” he asked.

“Better every day. Still on crutches, and griping about it constantly. But he should be good as new within the next few weeks….”

“Your sister? And DeDe?”

“Fine. Both of them. Just…fine.”

“Well. Good. That’s real good.”

Another silence. More staring.

"Coffee," she said finally, sounding downright desperate. "Would you—?"

"I'd love some." He looked relieved. "Yes."

She turned toward the kitchen area—and then stopped herself. "Wait."

"What?" Dark brows drew together.

"Jenny. You'll want to see Jenny…."

"I do. Very much. But isn't she sleeping?"

"God. I hope so."

Did he almost smile? It seemed he did. And then he suggested, "Maybe if we went in quietly…"

"Yes. Quietly. Good idea."

"I'll take off my shoes, why don't I?"

"Please."

He sat in the straight chair by the door, and removed his handmade Italian boots, setting them neatly out of the way. When he rose again, he waited for her to lead him down the hall.

In Jenny's darkened room, Hayley stood back by the rocker as he stepped up to the crib. Through the shadows, she watched him. He grasped the crib rail lightly. His head was tipped slightly down.

Jenny made a sound in her sleep, as if she were dreaming. And then she sighed.

It seemed to Hayley that Marcus smiled, but it was hard to tell for sure in the wedge of light that bled in through the half-open door to the hallway.

Finally, he turned to her. He lifted a hand and gestured toward the door. She followed him out, quietly pulling the door shut behind her.

They didn't speak until they reached the kitchen.

"She's bigger." He seemed surprised.

She shrugged. "Babies grow fast. And it's been weeks."

"Four weeks," he said.

She glanced at the clock. It was five past midnight. "And three days," she added. "As of five minutes ago."

"Too long," he said. His eyes were the deepest green right then. There was no mistaking the meaning of that look.

Relief, warm and sweet, went flooding through her.

He hadn't come to end it.

This was *not* goodbye.

But still, as swiftly as relief came over her, it fled. Could she have misread that look, after all?

She loved him so. And she wanted it to work out between them. That made her prone to read more into a tender expression than might actually be there.

It was altogether possible that he only meant he missed his daughter, that he hadn't been referring to her, to Hayley, at all.

Coffee. She'd offered him coffee. He lingered at the end of the counter as she got down the coffee beans and measured them into the grinder. The grinding sounded impossibly loud, and the silence when she finished, profound.

She poured the fresh grounds into the brew basket, filled the water reservoir, set the carafe in place and pushed the button, achingly aware as she performed each familiar movement, that he watched her.

Staring at the red brew light as the machine began to sputter, she cleared her tight throat and suggested, "We could sit. Until it's ready."

Neither of them moved.

She slanted him a glance. Yep. Watching.

He spoke at last. "You look good."

A short burst of laughter escaped her. "Oh, yeah. Fresh out of bed in my old robe and fuzzy slippers with my hair all over the place."

"That's right. You look beautiful." His voice was low, with a certain roughness in it now.

A tempting roughness.

He took a step toward her along the counter. Her body tightened. She made herself turn to face him fully, lifting her chin, letting the light of challenge gleam in her eyes. Her breath snagged in her throat as he stole another silent step.

Oh, yes. She was really starting to believe now.

This was *not* a man who'd come to say goodbye.

And oh, it had been forever. A lifetime, since she'd felt his hands, hungry and seeking, on her eager flesh.

They had so much to say to each other.

And yet, in that moment, she didn't give a damn for the words. She wanted the contact. Needed it. Craved it.

She wanted *him,* wanted Marcus. Touch to touch. Skin on skin.

Silent and sure on stocking feet, he approached. It was only a matter of two more steps and he was there, right in front of her.

The scent of him, so tempting and so well remembered, taunted her. He lifted a hand and touched her hair.

"God," he said. "Hayley…" Those green eyes scanned her face, hungry. Seeking.

"Yes," she whispered. "Oh, Marcus. Yes…"

"Sometimes I wondered if I'd ever touch you again…."

All she could manage was another yearning, breathless "Yes!"

He eased his fingers under her hair, curving them around her nape, brushing the tiny hairs there, sending hot shivers shimmering upward, over her scalp.

It was too much, the feel of his hand on her, at last. Too much—and never enough.

She surged up, pressed her mouth to his, parting her lips so she could taste him, lick him. He opened on a groan. She speared her tongue inside, tasting the sweetness, the heat, the wonder.

Feeding the fire.

His fingers slid boldly down the front of her, skimming her right breast, teasing the nipple to hardness. But only in passing.

His goal was the sash of her robe. He found it, grasped it and tugged. The sash came undone. She felt the front of the robe fall open.

She moaned as he followed her tongue back into her mouth. He sucked, sweet little tugs that beckoned, that teased, that set her aflame. He caught her top lip and drew on it, tongue sliding along the inner surface, thrilling her with its wet, rough glide. He guided her lower lip into position, and then he sucked it, too.

He pushed the robe off her shoulders. It fell to the floor with a tender little plopping sound. Under it, she had on her favorite old button-front nightshirt. And under that…

Nothing.

Except for his warm, big hand which immediately curved around the front of her right thigh, high up, beneath her frayed flannelette hem. His fingers dug in, so that she moaned and let her head drop back, losing the glorious wonder of his kiss.

"Closer," he muttered. "Closer to me…"

His free arm snaked around her and he pulled her body up against him, lifting her toes right off the floor. Her slippers slid off, one and then the other.

Bending her back, he nipped tender kisses,

from the hollow of her throat, up along her neck and over her chin. Then, at last, he took her mouth again, while the hand that cupped her thigh moved higher.

And higher still….

He curled those clever fingers around to the back, up high and tight, his index finger just brushing the moist curls that covered her sex.

She quivered in longing and anticipation, couldn't wait to drag him into the bedroom, whip out the protection her doctor had so thoughtfully provided, and take him deep inside her.

She clasped his shoulders, wiggling until he let her back down on her feet again, then trying to guide him backward, making hungry little moaning sounds, urging him to move.

He caught her lower lip between his teeth again. She whimpered some more.

He muttered, his voice rough velvet, "Uh-uh. Going nowhere. Not yet..."

He explored her, caressing fingers trailing upward, over the curve of her hip. She moaned into his mouth. He gave a low growl in response and clasped her waist, only to slip his hand fully between them and lay it, palm flat, on her belly, where she had held their child.

Below, she was melting, yearning, *dying* for more. For him never, ever to stop holding her, touching her, kissing her in that thorough, deep, overwhelming way.

She lifted her hips, ground them against him, felt the hard ridge that said how much he wanted her.

It was far too tempting, that ridge. She slipped her hand between them and eased it under his sweater. Grabbing his belt, she unhooked it in quick, eager moves. She had that buckle undone in no time and she slithered the belt off and away. The clasp made a sharp clinking sound as it hit the tile floor.

She undid the button at the top of his jeans. He helped her then, taking one side of the placket as she grabbed the other.

Together, they yanked that zipper wide. He groaned and worked his hips against her, wrapping his strong fingers around her wrist, guiding her hand where he wanted it, flat on his hard belly and then under the elastic of his boxers.

She found him, at last, so hot and hard and ready.

She wrapped her fingers around him and stroked him and he muttered her name against her parted lips, pleading in ragged whispers, "Yeah, like that. Hayley, oh, yeah…"

But then he stopped her, grabbing her wrist again, tighter than before, groaning low in his throat, pleading with her wordlessly.

She gave in and followed his lead. She knew him so well, after all. She understood that he wasn't ready yet, to let her have that much control over him, to let her take him all the way before he'd done as much for her.

She smiled a knowing smile against his mouth. "Too proud…"

"Uh-uh. Too eager. To touch you. To feel you come…" He covered her mouth in a searing kiss.

And his hand was up under her nightshirt again, touching her, petting her, those knowing fingers easing between her wet folds. Sensations—hot, melting, streaked with light, spun out from where he touched her. They claimed her whole body.

She cried out and her knees gave way. He supported her, kept her upright with his arm wrapped tight around her.

And he played her, fingers stroking her, in a rhythm that stole her breath and sent her mind reeling. Until she shattered, moaning, spangles of light behind her eyes, shimmers of wonder bursting at the center of her, sending glittery trails of purest pleasure singing along every nerve.

"I think I just died," she whispered, once the pleasure had crested and faded to a lovely, warm glow. She clutched his big shoulders. "Please don't let go of me. I'll melt into a puddle right here on the kitchen floor."

He made a low sound of satisfaction and nuzzled her neck. "Never," he vowed. "I'm never letting you go…."

The coffeepot gave a final sputter. "Just in

time," she told him with a breathless laugh. "Your coffee's ready."

He already had one hand at her back. He slipped the other under her knees and lifted her high. "It can wait." He turned and carried her out of the kitchen, across the living room and down the hall.

In her room, he set her gently on the bed.

He tugged on the hem of her sleep shirt. "I want you naked. Get this off…."

She lifted her arms and he whipped it away.

"Beautiful," he said, standing back a little, so he could see what he had revealed.

"Thank you." She gave him a tender smile. "You always say that, you know?"

"Because it's always true."

"Did I sound like I was complaining? I wasn't. I like it, when you call me beautiful."

"Good." The fly of his jeans still gaped wide.

He shoved them down, his boxers with them, skimming off both socks, as well.

"The sweater," she commanded, leaning back on her hands.

"You can be damn bossy, you know that?"

She didn't even try to deny it. "Just take off that sweater, just do what I say."

He took the sweater, pulled it up over his head, and tossed it somewhere behind him.

They regarded each other. She thought of how she loved this moment: the two of them, together. Naked.

It didn't get better than this.

But then he frowned. "Damn. I'm guessing it won't hurt you now, for us to be doing this."

"It's safe. I had my checkup last week."

"But what about protection? I don't have anything. And I have a feeling you don't really want to get pregnant tonight."

She already had the bedside drawer open and she held up the box of condoms. "Say thank you, Dr. Wright."

He wasn't frowning anymore. "A wonderful woman, that doctor of yours."

"Yes. Skilled. And thorough. Kind to her patients." She took out one of the pouches and set the box next to the bedside clock. "Not to mention, generous with the free samples." She reached out her arms for him.

He came down to her. She removed the condom from the pouch and slowly rolled it over him.

They stretched out, facing each other. He touched her, his palm skimming the swell of her hip.

"Too long, since we've been like this…" He said it softly, almost reverently.

She caressed his shoulder, loving the feel of

his smooth flesh, the hard muscle beneath. His body never failed to amaze her. He was beautifully formed. Even the thin, white scars that crisscrossed his strong back were dear to her. A mute testimony to his father's abuse, they showed what he'd endured.

"Much too long," she whispered. "Tell me this isn't a dream."

He trailed the back of his index finger downward, into the curve of her waist. "No dream. Real." He pulled her close.

They kissed. Endlessly.

And then, at last, the moment came. He rose above her. She took him inside, wrapping her legs around him. He braced himself on his fists, sparing her his full weight as he levered his hips more tightly to hers, so she felt him even more deeply than the moment before.

Stretched in the most luxurious way, filled

with him, she looked up into his eyes. Amazing. Nothing like it, to be joined with him. To be one with him in this intimate way.

She reached up, touched his face, traced the smooth, tempting softness of his warm lips. He kissed her fingers, sucked her thumb into his mouth.

Tears welled and escaped, twin trails along her temples.

Still, she hardly dared believe this was happening—the two of them, here, in her bed.

So often she'd dreamed of this moment. She *had* doubted, had wondered if they would ever share this bright magic again.

He bent close, whispered her name, kissed away the tear tracks, on one side of her face and then the other.

She smiled, nodded, so he would know she was okay. So he could rise above her again, and press in so tight and dear.

He moved within her. She picked up his rhythms and gave them back to him, lifting her hips to him, meeting each thrust.

He came down upon her, his hard chest crushing her breasts. But only to wrap her close and roll, giving her the top position.

She took control. Getting her knees under her, bracketing his lean hips with her soft thighs, she rode him. Her hands on his chest, her head thrown back, she took him deep. They stilled, pressed tight together. Until, slowly, she rose up, letting him out to the tip—and then taking him in all the way again.

He grasped her hips in his hands and he helped her—to rise until she almost lost him, to sink down upon him once more…and again.

And again, after that.

The rhythm claimed them. They gave themselves over to it. Her body was his and his body, hers.

She felt the end approaching, curling up like a high wave. And then rolling down, roaring like thunder as it came crashing through her. He surged up into her, holding her so tight against him.

Silence. A glowing stillness.

"Yes," she whispered, "Oh, yes…" The wave engulfed her, swallowed her. She went under gleefully, groaning his name.

Chapter Sixteen

From Jenny's room, they could hear the first fussy, questioning cries.

Hayley groaned and rubbed her cheek against the crisp dark hair on Marcus's chest. "Oh, no…"

He chuckled and the sound echoed pleasantly beneath her ear. He had his arms wrapped around her, secure and tight. "Hey. Her timing could have been worse."

The cries got louder.

Hayley blew out a breath. "Okay, okay… I'm coming…"

"I'll go with you."

She sat up and raked her hair back off her face. "I can do it." She slid away from him and rose to her feet beside the bed. "Go get your coffee." The door to the small master bath was only a few steps away. She went in there and shut the door.

A minute later, when she emerged, he was still stretched out on the bed, gloriously naked, those gorgeous muscular arms of his laced behind his head—and Jenny was still crying. "I *want* to go with you."

"Well, all right, then. Come on." She darted a glance around the room. "Where's my robe—and my slippers?"

"The kitchen, I believe."

She scooped up her nightshirt and pulled it on as Marcus got up, grabbed his jeans and took a quick turn in the bathroom. She went ahead to Jenny's room.

"Okay, okay. I'm here. Settle down."

Marcus appeared in the doorway. "That girl has a set of lungs on her."

"She's hungry." Hayley scooped up the squalling baby and started unbuttoning as she sat in the rocker. She put Jenny to her breast. Blessed silence descended. Hayley grinned up at Marcus, who stood by the crib. "Nothing so sweet as the sound of a baby *not* crying."

"I don't mind the crying."

"You've always been more patient than I am."

His eyes were moss-green right then. He approached. She tipped her face up to him as he touched her hair. "No. I don't think so. There's no one as patient as you."

The words seemed weighted with special meaning. She turned her face into his touch, so she could press her lips into the center of his palm.

He smiled at the kiss and then brushed the backs of his knuckles across her cheek. "I've missed you. Missed you so damn much." He curved his hand, so lightly, on Jenny's mostly bald head. "And her."

Hayley's throat clutched. She gulped to relax it. "I missed you, too."

"I should have come for you sooner, worked out all my old garbage sooner. I know it."

Her baby drew on her breast, the sensation, once so painful, brought only a glow of contentment now. "I was waiting," she said. "But I really didn't know what for. Somehow, I didn't expect you to come...."

"God. I hope you're glad that I did."

She nodded. "I am, Marcus. So very glad."

He was quiet. He seemed not to know what to say next.

She could relate to that. And it was okay with her. Sometimes it was hard to find the right words….

"I think I'll go get that coffee," he said.

"Good idea."

He left her.

Jenny finished at one breast and Hayley settled her at the other. Marcus came back. He stood over by the bureau, sipping from the red mug he'd claimed as his own back at Christmastime. When Jenny was through eating, Hayley rocked her until she needed changing.

"Let me…" Marcus set his mug on the bureau.

So Hayley handed Jenny over and left him to do diaper duty. She returned to her bedroom and sat on the edge of the bed.

Eventually, he came in and sat beside her. "She's asleep. Looking like an angel..."

Hayley nodded. "Yeah. No doubt about it. They're adorable when they're sleeping." She sent him a smile.

But he didn't see it. He was looking straight ahead, at the open door to the hallway. "I keep thinking I'm going to figure out how to say this...."

She didn't know what to tell him, how to encourage him. Since no words came, she put her hand on his knee and gave a reassuring squeeze.

He put his hand over hers. It felt so good. Cherishing. Right. He said, "I was furious, when you accused me of lying to you."

"Oh, yeah. I remember."

"You hit a nerve. Because I did lie. In more ways than just by not telling you that Adriana was after me again."

Hayley gulped and silently reminded herself, yet again, that she had to let him say this in his own way and in his own time. The urge was so powerful, to cut in, to start protesting that she didn't need to hear it, that it was all right. That he was here and she was glad he'd come for her and that was enough.

But it wasn't enough. She *did* need to hear it. Whatever it was. However much it hurt. She needed to hear—and he had to say it.

The truth was important. The truth, or rather, the lack of it, was the reason they'd just spent all these weeks apart. They'd come so far. No way could she let herself deny the truth now.

He said, "About two weeks ago, she started calling me again. I refused to take her calls. I erased her messages without even listening to them. Except for the first one, the one where she said that she knew you had left me and she couldn't wait for me to come to my senses so that she and I could pick up where we'd left off…."

Hayley had been staring at the door to the hallway. When his voice trailed off, she turned her head and met his waiting eyes.

"You okay?" He gave her hand a squeeze.

She blew out a breath. "I keep telling myself not to hate her. But I do. She betrayed you, left you flat, broke your heart so bad. Walked away without so much as a backward glance. She divorced you because she wanted to marry someone else…and now she waltzes back on the scene and can't understand what's wrong with you that you aren't waiting for her with open arms."

His mouth kicked up at one corner. "Yeah. Well. It never occurs to Adriana that things won't go her way. She wants what she wants when she wants it. And if she doesn't get what she wants, as a rule, there's hell to pay."

"Sheesh. Tell me about it."

"I'm trying to."

They both laughed then.

Hayley said, "Sorry. Continue. Please."

After a moment's thought, he did. "Last night, she came to the house. I took one look at her and I knew. I understood."

Hayley's heart started thumping as if it would beat its way out of her chest. She sucked in a slow breath. She waited for the worst.

He said, "I realized the truth. At last."

"Oh, God," she heard herself whisper on an indrawn breath.

And then he said, "I realized that I love *you,* Hayley. I've loved you for a damn long time. Since before you walked away from me last spring."

Her heart had stopped, just froze in midbeat. There was a rushing in her ears and her cheeks burned like hell's own fury. "I'm sorry. What did you say?"

He lifted her hand and he kissed it. "Damn it. I love you. *Have* loved you. You came into my life and you were—you *are*—like sunshine. Something bright and clean and sweet and good."

She swayed toward him. "Marcus?"

"Yeah?"

"Why didn't you tell me? Why didn't you just say so?"

He let go of her hand—but only to wrap his arm around her shoulder and draw her close against his side. "I thought I just explained that." Their lips were inches apart. She felt his breath, warm, scented of coffee, saw that shining rim of blue around the green of his eyes.

"I know you did," she whispered. "Tell me again."

"Because I'm too damn proud. Because I couldn't let myself admit how wrong I'd been, to think that what I'd had with Adriana was love. I didn't know squat about love. Didn't know what the real thing could be. Until you."

She rested a hand on his warm chest, felt the strong, even beat of his heart beneath her palm. "Oh, see. Now, I am really liking the sound of this."

He stole a quick, sweet kiss. "I had a feeling you might."

"So…as soon as you saw Adriana again, *that's* when you knew that you loved me?"

"That's right."

"Life is so strange sometimes."

"It damn sure is."

"You probably should have agreed to see her

sooner. It would have saved us both a whole lot of misery."

"Yeah. If I'd only known."

"Oh, Marcus. I love you, too."

He curled a finger under her chin. "I know you do. And I love to hear you say it."

"I'll never stop saying it."

"Good. It's a fine thing for a man to hear—when the right woman says it."

"I love you, love you, love you, love you." She clasped his shoulder and brought her mouth right up to his. "Now's the moment you should kiss me."

"My pleasure."

He claimed her lips. She sighed and opened. It was a perfect kiss. Slow and deep and wet, full of heat and tenderness. A kiss that promised a lifetime of joy. And truth. And mutual trust.

When he lifted his mouth from hers, she let out a happy sigh. They dropped back across the bed in unison, and turned their heads to grin at each other.

He said, “So I’m hoping this means you’ll come home with me now.”

“Oh, yes. Absolutely. We love each other. And we’re a family, you and Jenny and me. Of course I’ll come home with you. Now I know you’re mine, that you’re with me and you’ve got no doubts, I can handle anything. Even that ex of yours, if I have to.”

“I don’t think Adriana will be bothering us anymore.”

“Well, we can hope,” she teased.

“Seriously. After last night, I don’t think she’ll be coming around. I think she finally got the message—and yeah, I know. With her, you can never be absolutely sure. But I know she heard me loud and clear when I told her that I love you. I asked her not to bother us anymore."

"And…?"

"She said she would leave us alone."

"Wow."

They grinned at each other, both of them more than satisfied.

She scooted closer. "I don't think I've ever been happier."

"Good."

"Also, my feet are freezing."

"Then let's get under the covers."

He took off his jeans and she got rid of her nightshirt and they snuggled up under the blankets together. He gathered her close. She tucked herself against him, her hand curled near his heart, her head beneath his chin.

She closed her eyes. She had it all. Everything she'd ever wished for, during all the

Christmases of her lonely childhood. She had a family—a sister and a brother, a sweet little niece and a whole bunch of Bravo relatives all over the country.

She had Marcus and Jenny. She belonged to them and they belonged to her.

"Dreams do come true," she whispered drowsily.

He made a low noise of agreement and she felt his lips brush the crown of her head.

Home in her husband's loving arms at last, Hayley sighed in contentment and drifted off into a deep and peaceful sleep.

* * * * *